George W. Warder

Eden Dell

Love's Wanderings

George W. Warder

Eden Dell
Love's Wanderings

ISBN/EAN: 9783337195243

Printed in Europe, USA, Canada, Australia, Japan

Cover: Foto ©Andreas Hilbeck / pixelio.de

More available books at **www.hansebooks.com**

Very Truly
Geo. W. Warder
ATT'Y AT LAW

"All things beautiful and tender
Summer bloom, and sunset skies,
Wear alone their Eden splendor
In the light of loving eyes."
Hathaway.

"One divine caress,
One blessed moment of forgetfulness
I've found within those arms, and that shall lie
Shrined in my souls deep memory till I die."
Moore.

KANSAS CITY:

PRESS OF RAMSEY, MILLETT & HUDSON.

1878.

I weave a chaplet from the years
  All fashioned by the hand of Fate.
I read a lesson from the spheres
Whose mission is to never wait
That God hath written on time's page
That ACTION is the law of life,
And man from youth to hoary age
A living struggle warm with strife.

THIS VOLUME IS AFFECTIONATELY DEDICATED, BY THE
AUTHOR TO HIS SAINTED WIFE. THE CHARM OF WHOSE
GRACE AND CHARACTER, THE NOBILITY AND LOVELINESS OF WHOSE
LIFE, IS ENSHRINED IN HIS HEART, AND HALLOWED IN HIS MEMORY.
WHOSE ANXIOUS SOLICITUDE, AND UNSELFISH DEVOTION FOR THE
WELFARE OF OTHERS MADE HER THE IMPERSONATION OF LOVE
AND DUTY, AND THE SYNONYM OF TRUTH AND GOOD-
NESS. THROUGH HER UNTIMELY LOSS HE FEELS
THAT LIFE IS UNSATISFYING, YOUTH A DELUSION,
MIDDLE AGE A STRUGGLE, AND OLD AGE A
REGRET. TO PRESERVE SOME HAL-
LOWED MEMORIES THIS BOOK IS
PUBLISHED: FOR THE PAST
HATH ITS MEMORIES, THE
PRESENT ITS DUTIES,
THE FUTURE HATH HOPE,
WHICH LOOKS UP TO
THE STARS, AS
THE GOLDEN
STEPPING STONES
ALONG THE PATHWAY OF
IMMORTALITY, WHERE THE IS-
LANDS OF THE BLESSED SMILE IN
PERENNIAL BEAUTY, AND OUR LOVED
SHALL GREET US ON THE BLISSFUL
SHORES OF THE DEATHLESS ETERNITIES.

In all God's million starry spheres,
Stand forth no truer, nobler peers
Than God's image wrapt in hopes and fears ;
 A worthy man, a lovely woman.
From satelite to central sun,
From angels lost to heavens won,
God ne'er hath blent two hearts as one
So near divine, so grandly human.

God's will ; man should not dwell alone,
But woman's worth and beauty own,
And climb up to her love, as to a throne :
 His heart's best true evangel,
He found that nature, ease and art,
Were not enough to nobly start,
The true soul fires, but " sad the heart
That knows no earthly angel."

The gentle faith, the noble worth,
Of one beloved o'er all the earth,
With graceful charm sat at his hearth ;
 His sweetest dearest dream of heaven.
Thy truthful merit could he sing,
He'd seek the harp and angel wing,
Of love's lost jewel heaven could bring,
The cherub from thy bosom riven.

CONTENTS.

HEART THROBS.   PAGE.

MY SAINTED WIFE 9
KISS OUR DARLING AND COME AWAY 13
I TURN ANOTHER LEAF OF TIME 15
OUR LOVED AND LOST 22
A DISTANT VIEW 24
SLEEP, DEATH AND OBLIVION 28
MIND 32
LOVE 38

EDEN DELL, OR LOVE'S WANDERINGS.

CANTO I—THE PARTING 47
"   II—FOREWARNED, A PROPHECY 56
"   III—FOUL PLAY BENEATH THE STARS 69
"   IV—RETRIBUTION, OR THE VIGILANTES 75
"   V—RECOVERED—A SCENE OF JEALOUSY 84
"   VI—AMBUSHED—A SAD DISCOVERY . . 97
"   VII—A RIVAL AND A FRAUD 104
"   VIII—THE CAPTIVES, ... 115
"   IX—HIDDEN VALLEY—AT THE STAKE 122
"   X—THE AGED CHIEF,—A LEGEND 130
"   XI—THE RESCUE AND THE RED PALADINS 139
"   XII—WHAT SHADOWS WE ARE—A EUROPEAN TOUR . 147
"   XIII—WHAT SHADOWS WE PURSUE—WRECKED . . . 165
"   XIV—A RETURN—A FAREWELL 182
"   XV—MISFORTUNES—A DIGRESSION 194
"   XVI—THREE FRIENDS HAVE MET AGAIN 205

CANTO XVII—UTOPIAN DREAMS AND LOTUS LEAVES 214
"   XVIII—TRIED—PURIFIED—A COINCIDENT 226
"   XIX—TWO SCENES AND A CHAPTER 239
"   XX—MOUNTAIN MEADOW MASSACRE 259
"   XXI—THE SPANISH MAID—AN EPISODE . . 271
"   XXII—THE WEDDING—EDEN REBUILT 290

WAYWARD FANCIES.

TWO STRANGER GUESTS 305
A LEGEND OF THE DELUGE 320

FOOTPRINTS AND SHADOWS.

WOMAN 329
TO VIRGINIA—REMEMBRANCE 331
TO ETTIE, THE ROSEBUD OF THE HILLSIDE 332
ETTIE, THE ROSEBUD, HAS PERISHED 334
LAST WORDS OF STONEWALL JACKSON 338
DEATH OF GENERAL J. C. BRECKINRIDGE 341
CENTENNIAL THANKS 344
THE DAY COMETH, ALSO THE NIGHT 347
THE PAST AND FUTURE 349
THE MINSTREL'S FAREWELL 353

HEART THROBS.

We live for love in whole or part.
The inspiration of all Art
    Is love. 'Tis labor's best reward:
    The alchemy of **joy :** life's lord :
Earth's only heaven **from above.**
To those that live **a smile of love**
    Is like the laurel to the brave,
    Worth countless garlands on their grave.

Think not love's labor e'er was lost,
It built creation without cost
    To frugal man, and named him lord :
    T'was hate brought strife and dark discord
And God will wipe love's sinless tears :
Like truth, she hath eternal years.

MY SAINTED WIFE.

Thou angel of my better world,
Where joy and peace her flag unfurled
Beside my hearth!   Thou love impearled
    Upon my life!
Deep where the heart throbs rise and swell,
I feel the witchery and the spell
Of thy fair face I loved so well—
    My darling wife.

The magic of thy lovely smile
The very angels would beguile,
And thrill their golden harps awhile
    With sweeter life.
So tender, loving, true and kind,
So faithful, gentle and refined
Each impulse of thy heart and mind—
    My noble wife.

Can I forget the charm and grace
Of loveliness that stamped thy face,

2

And crowned thee noblest of thy race,
　　In death or life?
Can I forget thy faith and trust
In God and Heaven?　And can or must
I deem this providence wise or just—
　　My angel wife!

All silent as the voiceless night,
With folded hands on **breast of white**,
In pallid **shroud!**　O God, the sight!
　　No pulse of breath.
As white as snows **on mountain crest**,
The cross of flowers upon thy breast,
Thy weary, helpless hands are pressed
　　Cold, cold in death.

O rise and stay! Go not away!
God sent thee on thy bridal day
To be my angel 'mid earth's fray—
　　My love, my life.
O! one more smile my grief to 'suage,
One word of love upon life's page,
To cheer me to decrepid age—
　　From thee, my wife!

I kissed the forehead, cold and fair,
I smoothed the glossy braids of hair,
I bowed my soul in anguished prayer,
　　That she might live.

"O spare my precious, noble wife,
My patient martyr weak from strife :
Restore the angel of my life—
      Give back! O give!"

Alas too late! too late! too late!
I've felt the dreaded hand of fate.
I can but mourn and sigh and wait—
      My sainted wife.
Beside her cherub boy we laid
Her form to rest beneath the shade,
Where dust is heaped with silent spade—
      The close of life.

As slowly sifts life's ebbing sand,
On memory's hights I gaze and stand,
And reach to grasp thy vanished hand—
      My angel wife.
Farewell! I cannot count the cost
Of what I've suffered, loved and lost,
I drift a barque, lone, tempest-tossed
      The sea of life.

Thy love hath cheered me on thus far
As fair and perfect as a star,
Which naught on earth could change or mar,
      The solace of my life.
But life is short.   Soon on that shore
Where Stygian waves are crossed no more

I'll greet the angel I adore—
    My sainted wife.

Beyond where flows the restless tide
Of earthly grief, and joy and pride,
Thee and thy angel boy beside—
    Thou sleepest well.
But where life's changeful billows toss
Thy babe and I must mourn thy loss;
Must taste what pain, and bear what cross—
    But God can tell.

Ere passed thy life another came,
A fledgling fair, to bear thy name
And wear thy pure, unsullied fame,
    I pray and trust,
For her, for thee, with sad refrain,
With sighing harp to soothe my pain
I'd link thy life without a stain,
    To fame most just.

I fear not what may be my lot,
My name may rest unknown, forgot,
But thine unsullied with a spot
    Of fault or blame,
Should live renewed in heart and brain,
A consecrated shade and fane
Wherever love and duty reign,
    Or truth has name.

KISS OUR DARLING AND COME AWAY

Dead!   Our darling is dead, dear wife,
His angel spirit has heavenward fled :
His little feet will no longer tread
The rugged paths of this sorrowing life.
    Kiss his forehead of marble clay,
    Kiss our darling and come away.

Fair was his lovely form, dear wife,
Bright and sunny his cherub face :
See what a dimple the angels did trace,
When they kissed him first on the shores of life.
    Kiss him again, for only to-day
    Can you kiss our darling and come away.

Sweet was his lovely smile, dear wife,
Mild and beaming his eyes of blue;
Fair as the sun, when on diamonds of dew
He climbs the morn of a new waking life.
    Kiss our darling—this form is but clay,
    The casket is left, but the jewel's away.

The casket is left—even it will not stay
So perfectly chiseled, so white and so fair ;

Sure death cannot spoil so perfect a prayer,
And beauty'll unnerve the dark hand of decay.
　　O, fair dimpled hands! how sweetly ye lay!
　　Folded forever, dear wife come away.

The jewel's departed—the mystery of soul,
Borne swift through nebulous mists afar,
Rejoices an angel upon a bright star,
Where dark tides of sorrow and death never roll.
　　"Come, fairest floweret," the Savior did say,
　　"Where frosts wither not and storms never stray."

"Dear wife, look up to the isles of the blest,
　　Where joyous and happy his spirit hath fled,
　　Though the form it may moulder, the soul is not dead,
　　But pass'd to its home of bliss and sweet rest.
　　　Weep not so bitterly, know that to-day
　　　Thy darling's in heaven, so, wife, come away."

The parents they turned from their sweet, dead child,
And all earth seemed so dreary and cold,
It held not a treasure, their arms could enfold.
So dear as the charm of his fair angel smile.
　　O, kiss him, and tear your sad hearts away,
　　A fair little form seeks its chamber of clay.

I TURN ANOTHER LEAF OF TIME.

The sun, wrapt in his mantle red,
    Sinks down behind the crimson West,
The moon comes from her orient bed,
    With silver dripping from her crest;
The stars peep through the vault of night,
    Like distant hopes that come to cheer
The wanderer with new beams of light
    From some unknown and brighter sphere.

The night is fair, the air is chill,
    A snowy mantle from the skies
Enwraps the earth, so white and still,
    It seems a robe of paradise.
The heaven bends down her starry vault,
    Like memory weeping o'er a grave
Where vanished souls, like stars, are set.
    And dreaming of a voice to save.

I, musing, turn a leaf of time
    Here in the twilight of the year,
While listening to the solemn chime
    Of memories sadder than a tear;

I gaze toward **the golden heights**
  Of far-off isles, beyond the shore,
And kiss again, in fancy's flights,
  The face that I shall see no **more.** .

The **spring** brought forth **a tender bloom,**
  That **summer** kissed with fragrant **breath,**
But ah! the autumn draped his tomb,
  And winter was the chill of death.
As seasons swiftly follow each,
  So death pursues the steps of life,
And nature hath a silent speech—
  The soul that thinks is full of strife.

" We live, we die." Is that the end
  Of our immortal longings here?
And can **this** little sentence penned
  Sum up life's heart-ache and its cheer?
Can joy tread on the heels of grief,
  Can sorrow lift the troubled soul,
And bid death turn another leaf
  When time has folded up its scroll?

Love's jewels gathered in **our arms,**
  Our loved, that have been. shall they **be ?**
Sure **souls have** their immortal charms,
  And there's a time when we shall see .
I span the space from **now** till then.
  And. in the vision of the mind.

I lift the vail of human ken.
  To find the blind but lead the blind.

Yet, in my dreams of grief and love,
  A hope looms like a mountain grand.
Where, from its Pisgah heights above,
  I view another promised land.
I catch a glimpse of sun-lit truth
  Beyond where constellations shine,
Where souls shall taste the fount of youth.
  Sprung from the breast of love divine.

This leaf of time, so sadly turned,
  Is moist with many a falling tear:
These solemn lessons. deeply learned.
  Are written on the vanished year;
And, gazing on its checkered page,
  The scenes that were come not again,
Unless fond memory bring them up
  To stir another sea of pain.

A streamlet from the lake divine
  Burst forth within the vale below;
Fresh from the hand of God it smiled
  And laughed beneath the sunrise glow.
I marked it oft, I loved it well,
  Its sunny, glowing smile to me
Was sweeter than the joyous swell
  Of music rippling o'er the sea.

It was a well-spring of **bright love**
  That bubbled through the shadowed vale,
And caught the sunlight from above,
  Where joy could spread her buoyant sail.
But on a golden summer **eve**
  A shadow fell,—I watched, **I feared,**
And while my soul was bent with grief,
  The golden streamlet disappeared.

I wrestled with a hopeless strife—
  Pain set her mark upon my soul,—
For death had **stole a** bud of **life**
  That time can **never more unfold.**
Now climbing slow the hills of faith
  I see the golden streamlet run,
Beyond the heights that girt the vale,
  And smile beneath a brighter sun.

It sifted through **the** golden sands,
  'Twas purged from all the dross of earth ;
Beyond the vale where sorrow stands,
  It dwells a fount of fadeless worth.
And yet I know the mists will rise
  Before the dawn, beyond the night,
When I shall know **to** love is wise.
  Affection is all true delight.

I've marked the bounds of pleasure's flight,
  I've counted merit o'er and o'er,

The wise may reason wrong or right,
    The fool may hoard his paltry store,
But God has set the seal of fate.
    True wealth is only of the soul.
And they who dote on earth's estate
    Must taste where bitter waters roll.

I am not what I will to be,
    I reach to grasp a higher aim,
To climb the sun-lit heights and see
    The hopes and promises I claim.
I gird my soul with strong resolve
    To bear the griefs that time shall cost,
And trust the ages will evolve
    That love, true love, is never lost.

I muse upon that long ago
    I tore an image from my breast,
And now the heart that's sad and sore
    Must fold another love to rest.
And still I dream that yet, that yet,
    The hopes that are beyond recall,
We'il see where suns shall never set
    And sorrow's shadows never fall.

O, little darling! wast thou sent
    To lead us to the God above?
For where thy angel spirit went
    There is the heaven of our love.

If e'er within the golden gate
   I wander by the crystal sea,
O, shall I meet thee, know thy fate?
   Else would it be a heaven to me?

Thy only mark upon earth's breast
   Sleeps in the pallid, cold moonlight;
A little grave with snow-robed crest
   That peers into the void of night.
It holds the bright and laughing eyes,
   The dimpled cheeks that I have kissed,
The angel face I loved to prize,
   The cherub form so long we've missed.

But not thy stainless spirit? no,
   I ask where, whither has it flown?
From star to star, from sun to sun,
   Until it reached its Maker's throne?
A voice from out the ages spoke
   From where the burning suns are fed,
"Gird up thy loins, go forth in hope,
   The living yet shall see their dead."

O soul! O harp of thousand strings!
   Oft hath a vanished finger swept
Thy wondrous chords; and angel wings
   Have rustled in thy listening sleep,
Where silence was unuttered thought,
   That to the hungry spirit given,

The melodies of earth were caught
  And blended with the dream of heaven.

O yearning memories, sad and grand!
  Prophetic of a time to be.
O wanderer on a lonely strand
  That gazes o'er a boundless sea!
Know many souls in all the past
  Have dreamt love opes all doors and bars
Beyond the sun-set shores at last,
  Where islands glitter like the stars.

How many leaves the book of time
  Shall open to my future view,
How many hills of strife to climb
  I know not, wish not now I knew.
I gather up new hope and trust
  As soldiers cloak their martial forms,
And face the future that I must,
  In faith abide the coming storms.

OUR LOVED AND LOST.

Is there no bright, unfading clime,
  Beyond this world of severed ties,
To fill the wants that mock in time,
  And dry the tears from sorrow's eyes?
Where blast of winter never blows,
  And endless spring brings deathless flowers:
Where we may see the face of those
  We loved in this sad world of ours?

Is there no pure, immortal sphere
  Beyond this realm of fleeting time,
Where hopes and fears that mock us here
  Will blossom into bliss sublime?
Where ceaseless joys on angel's wing,
  With golden harps shall chase the hours,
And we shall hear the dear ones sing
  Who loved us in this world of ours.

The summers bloom, the autumns fade,
  And winters blow along our way,
And 'mid earth's changing light and shade
  Are memories of those passed away,
They come amid our griefs and pain,
  Like songs we've heard in days gone by,

Whose murmurs, like the distant main,
  Grow loudest when the storms are nigh.

Bright laurels fade and honors rust,
  And oft our barque is tempest-tossed,
And willows wave above the dust
  Of those whom we have loved and lost.
Yet, in our bright and saddest dream,
  Their silent forms we often see,
Like shadows floating o'er time's stream,
  Cast from the vast eternity.

The flowers of springtime in their turn
  Bloom in fresh beauty o'er the lea,
And brightest stars that set, return.
  And view their faces in the sea.
Beyond the sunset and the night,
  Where pain and sorrow has no power,
Our loved and lost shall greet our sight
  When we close life's transient hour.

There is a fair, perennial world,
  Where hopes and joys that mock us here
Will lift their banners high unfurled
  To music of that blissful sphere,
And there our souls with rapture greet,
  'Mid anthems of bright rolling hours.
With folded wings in converse sweet.
  Those we loved in this world ours.

A DISTANT VIEW.

Methought upon time's farthest verge,
   Within the range of countless worlds,
I saw the ceaseless ages surge,
   And suns like mazy snowflakes whirled ;
And, standing on the farthest star
   That decks creation's realms so wide,
I viewed the rolling earth afar
   In all its pomp of death and pride.

I saw it spin through realms of space
   And circle fleetly round the sun,
And changing seasons quickly chase
   Each other o'er the path she run.
Dipped half in darkness, half in light,
   As whirling on her poles she flew,
Till, lessening, as a bird in flight,
   She faded from my wistful view

" It was the vast Eternity,"
   I, musing, said, and thought I knew,
That drank her in its shoreless sea,
   As ocean drinks a drop of dew.

Methought is this the solid earth
  On which I trod with joyous feet,
And was it spoken into birth
  To fade with worlds my vision greet?

Is man the creature of an hour,
  An insect of a summer day,
Decked with the gaudy show of power,
  And wrapped with pride that sinks to clay?
Is that his home, his life, his all,
  Where, with the bubbling toys of time,
He feebly treads a crusted ball,
  Nor looks, nor soars to worlds sublime?

O man, with crouching spaniel heart!
  With lust of wealth and bounded brain,
Is there no high and noble art
  To ease the "world's immortal pain?"
When viewed from o'er the realms of space,
  Passion's candle dimmed, and on the shelf,
How groveling seems that noble race
  Smote by the "dark disease of self."

Man's soul is like the rolling world,
  Dipped half in darkness, half in light,
And each with maddening speed is whirled
  To brightest day or darkest night.
One view has gladness and the sun,
  One darkness and the somber dream.

And passion marks the course they run,
  And life is like a turbid stream.

Strong passions lose their power to please,
  Joy sickening, drops her sweetest charm,
Nor balmy sleep the bosoms ease
  Where grief has showed its power to harm.
Oblivion sweeps not o'er the past,
  And memory oft times has a sting,
Affection's jewels will not last,
  And hope sometimes forgets to sing.

" What, then, is earth, and what is man?"
  I ask, in gloomy thought and pride,
As on the viewless star I stand,
  And view the countless worlds so wide.
Sure, it is but a meteor bright
  That shoots awhile through ether clear,
And man upon it sinks from sight
  As earth drinks up a falling tear.

A lofty scorn I dared to cast
  On human passions, hopes and fears,
Because afar the world had past;
  I stood beyond the rolling years.
But humbled is my gloomy pride;
  With bended head I hide my grief,
Nor seek to mock time's rolling tide,
  Nor scorn life's fleeting years so brief.

Contentment is the home we need,
    With will to work and patient wait.
And faith will give us wings of speed.
    And hope will sweeten cruel fate,
And love will bring us golden bliss,
    And heal the bleeding wounds of earth:
And in a fairer world than this
    We'll bloom in bright and endless birth.

A prisoner in earth's wintry waste,
    I'll find enough of fleeting breath
To plume time's wing with gentle haste,
    Nor fear the hungry eyes of death.
I'll think and soar on fearless wing
    While others grovel in the dust,
And faith will tune the song I sing—
    In God and Heaven shall be my trust.

SLEEP, DEATH AND OBLIVION.

Sleep, that smooths the rugged brow of care,
  That fans with zephyrs from an angel's wing,
That o'er the mind, with softness of the balmy air,
  Does her dark mantle of deep silence fling—
That checks the heated flow of burning thought,
  And cools it with the waters from a mossy spring,
Until it drinks the shadows that are brought,
  And fades into the twilight that its soothings bring—
Sleep, that wraps the world in darkness dim and deep,
  Yet, all unseen, and felt alone in that we feel it not:
All else has something of a touch, but balmy sleep
  It steals our senses, and we know it not.

We walk like spectres through its silent shades,
  Nor feel its spongy soil beneath our tread,
But the closing daylight and the darkness fades,
  And by oblivion's fabled waters we are led.
Yet oft we journey through its dreamy land,
  As though it were a world of motion and of light,
And in its visions, joy and sorrow take our hand,
  As though our mind looked through the doors of sight.
It is the soothing balm and solace of a restless world,
  Which else would roll in madness and despair.

Men would pray for it, as for the sun if hurled
  From his bright chariot in the fields of air.

This angel sleep, that brings us sweet repose,
  That blunts the edge of grief, and from heaven unfurled
Lets down our loved ones, silent uprose,
  And led me down into its lower world,
When lo! I stood beside a silent creeping stream,
  That through a land of gloomy twilight stole:
Its sombre cliffs stood deep and dark in dream,
  The stream slid on, nor did its drowsy waters roll,
But glided smooth, unruffled as the flowing oil,
  And slipped 'twixt gloomy cliffs, with dismal crest,
On which stood pines unvexed by breeze; and on its soil
  The poppies droop—the winds were folded on its breast.

" Is this oblivion's stream? I asked of sleep,
  Are these the waters of the fabled Lethe?
And o'er whate'er they darkly sweep
  The past is lost and buried far beneath—
Where sweet or sad forgetfulness is found,
  Where men who've searched in near and distant lands
And after treading restless earth around,
  Have lifted here their pale, beseeching hands,
And found forgetfulness?" But sleep silent stood,
  With eyes still closed, and then I asked again,
"And why should men forget? Is there some blood
  That cries from earth, like Abel's 'gainst a Cain?

Is Lethe the fabled fancy of a feverish brain,
  Invented, when the gory hand of cruel deeds
Was shaken in man's face by victims slain—
  When remorse, like a vulture, on his memory feeds?"
But methought sure sleep gives peace and rest,
  And for a time forgetfulness.   And then I look,
And lo! the earth was lying in sleep's breast,
  As a sick, moaning child whom peace and rest forsook.
"Have men drank poison, and can sleep no more?
  Is it the restless longings of the soul, or cares of life,
The sting of conscience, or proud thoughts that soar?
  Must man e'en in his dreams mix in hot strife?

Then, where's forgetfulness?"   with anxious heart
  Again I asked, that I may bring it to the upper earth;
That it may still life's pangs, and soothe pain's smart;
  That men may dwell in peace, with quiet mirth.
When lo! I saw, but just beyond, a stream,
  Whose dark and chilly gloom did make me start.
'Twas deep and narrow, and o'er it light nor shadows gleam,
  So dark the gloom ; and cold, as if from heart
Of more than thousand icebergs.   I knew 'twas death.
  I saw the grim, wan ferryman, with his shadow boat,
Like spectres glide, freighted with mortal's breath—
  With silent oars and deathly stillness did it float.

Methought, here man is your oblivion of life,
  This narrow stream will wash out all your fears,

Your loves and joys and dark and restless strife.
   Here you'll forget earth's pains, and toils, and tears.
Methinks I've learned this in sleep's shadowy deep,
   These silent streams are not so far apart,
And death may have its dreams like sleep.
   Sleep stills the mind, death stills the heart—
They are twin brothers. One, lasts in time;
   The other, we know not how long it lasts;
But each locks up our senses in an unknown clime—
   The one builds up the body that the other blasts.

Sleep, death and oblivion, are things that mock;
   Sleep, in dreams; death and oblivion, in the grave;
And yet we are not mocked. We only walk
   Amid realities that bind us like a slave.
Sleep soothes and cheers; death grimly reaps and slays.
   It makes earth but a tomb—its house of revelry;
It stalks amid life's dark and brightest ways
   And takes its victims. All are 'neath its slavery.
With chilling frosts it nips life's brightest flowers,
   And with pale faces and a gasp they go,
And vaguely trust to bloom 'neath other bowers,
   Where death's grim hand will never blast them so.

MIND.

Hail, invisible spirit! immortal essence of Divinity,
  Creative breath that breathed upon cold, sluggish clay,
And every atom felt the warm and thrilling touch of in-
    ward Deity—
  A central, all-pervading presence, a bright and glowing
    ray
Of heaven-sent light, and hope, and joy, and swelling life,
  That thrills and trembles through its conscious being,
Like the tremulous silver of the sea in gentle strife
  That waves and sparkles in the sun and breeze.

God breathed on clay and man became a living soul,
  'Tis God in man—a spark struck from omniscient life,
That, radiating from its central source, does warm the
    whole,
  And give new touch and feeling to unconscious dust;
To the dull habiliments that wrap its viewless form,
  And down receding time does hold its life and power,
Its essence fadeless, and its being indestructible as the
    breath
  Of Deity that gave it birth, and smiled upon its natal
    hour.

Incomprehensible, yet comprehending more than aught
    besides;
  Viewless as the shifting air, yet viewing things visible
    and unseen;
Swayed by volitions that surge through all its depths like
    tides:
  Whispering intuitions, feeling thoughts, and weighing
    what they mean.
Like Deity, a viewless eternal spirit, yet not like it unborn
  And uncreated. Thou wast created by the Uncreated,
And wrapt in finite dust—mortal in all through which
    thou manifests thyself,
  Yet feeling an inborn power, an endless birth, progres-
    sive and imperishable.

That spark once struck from Deity—breathed from His
    breath—
  That made one living man, divisible, yet unimpaired,
Has thrown off other sparks of vitalizing breath,
  Until that uncreated creating breath has brought forth
    millions,
Peopled nations, and the realm of spirits beyond the
    stream of death.
  God made but two: it was enough to people endless
    worlds
Ne'er trod by living feet, or swept by wing of soaring
    spirits,
  Through all the cycles of immeasurable duration as they
    ceaseless whirl.

The casket of decay **that wraps** this fadeless gem,
  Like solid substance **all,** does perish with the use,
And weighs this essence down, like monarch's head is
      bowed by diadem:
  And shackles it like slave condemned to toil beneath a
    ' **heavy** chain,
So that it cannot soar to whence it came—and **soon**
  Must go—to viewless realms where spirits reign.
Yet warm and glowing, **as the sun** at **noon,**
  It makes this **casket thrill with** intense **joy** or pain.

And from its living centre **wildly sweep**
  Bright burning thoughts, sensations **soft or** sharp,
That tremble on the nerves with feeling deep,
  Until they quiver at its touch, **like** strings **upon a** harp,
And sweet or saddest music swells through all the chambers
  Of this wondrous mechanism **of** creative **power.**
And wears it till it can not hold **its** panting prisoner,
  Then takes **its** flight, and leaves it as **a** ruined tower—

Crumbling and time-worn to fall and moulder **to decay—**
  Lone and silent, deserted by its lordly guest,
That **once** upon **a** checkered summer day
  Did **tread** its joyous halls, **then with** beauty blest.
The **link once** broken **or severed by** time's rust,
  That binds the immortal **to its** "mortal coil"—
That strange, connecting **link** between mind and dust,
  No hand can forge again the brittle link by science, art
    or toil?

Though clothed upon, and shackled down, yet still
  It soars through all the doors of thought and sense,
And sees, and hears, and action does its dwelling fill;
  It sweeps far out into the realm of other worlds:
It looks on matter with a calculating eye;
  It weighs it—treads amid the stars that glitter as they
      whirl—
Measures the all-dazzling sun that sweeps above the vault-
      ed sky,
  With all its retinue of worlds that circle round it as
      they fly.

It tracks the comet as it shoots upon its burning course;
  It sails through space upon the wings of air, and by a tire-
      less force—
A magic sweep of fancy's touch it views bright scenes far o'er
      the deep.
  By subtle power it traces matter to its elemental source,
Nor knows its bounds, but seeks o'er all the universe and
      time to leap.
  Like its Father Spirit it moves on chaos, and it turns to
      light;
It smiles upon the world, and life and joy like flowers spring
      up,
  And matter feels its subtle essence, and morning dawns
      above the night.

'Tis part of Deity, and as immortal as its creative God.
  Death is but a shadow 'cross its path of destiny.

To the soul there is no grave; the tomb can not grasp its
      viewless form;
  Earth is but its birth-place—the cradle of its infancy—
Where it drops its cumbrous wrappings for the wings of im-
      mortality.
    Time, the vestibule of eternity, is where it points its
      course, and takes its leap
Into the vast unknown, toward the Infinite and Eternal, and
      sweeps
  Out upon its endless progression in knowledge and perfec-
      tion through immensity of worlds.

This thing invisible is greater than the visible, the unseen
      than the seen;
  You cannot nail it to the cross, or puncture it with a spear.
It can soar untrammeled, where matter ne'er has been.
  Once created, ne'er uncreated, in time, eternity, far or
      near;
It must exist. The creative will that kindled it to birth
  Can ne'er blast its glowing life, nor quench it in the ocean
      of His wrath;
The distant stars may fall, and nations perish from the earth;
  World upon worlds may vanish from their glowing path;

Man may sink to dust, and all the living moulder in the
      tomb;
  Time and eternity may perish in their onward flight;
Earth may melt, the sun may crumble into specks of gloom,
  And darkness wrap the universe in chaos, death and night;

Yet the thinking part, the soul eternal, the quenchless mind,
  Shall live in endless life, undimmed by age and death,
And in the far-reaching, ceaseless ages, still shall find,
  It has a self-existent life, beyond time's fleeting breath.

LOVE.

Could I but mould the vault on high,
I'd blazon *Love* upon the sky
  Imprint it on the dazzling sun,
  And every life when first begun.
Pour it a song through coming years
Blent with the music of the spheres,
  A voice to keep the worlds from strife,
  The poetry of joy and life.

Love gives our lives a richer health,
Love adds unto our souls new wealth,
  It steps into the heart, when lo!
  New streams of joy begin to flow.
We see more wealth in one bright eye
Than in the proud and jeweled sky
  Of golden stars; than in the deep
  Rich bosom of the sea where sleep
The continents of glittering pearl,
And the lost riches of a world.

Man may his warmth of nature hide,
And chill it with a freezing pride,

Erase from life affections port,
Be traffics ship, ambitions sport,
Yet in his secret soul will smile
Affection's sun, love's starry isle;
　Where he will wander when the soul
　Is sad with strife and sorrows roll.
There love will ope the doors and bars
To isles that glitter like the stars.

Love is the home-land of the soul,
Beyond where glowing planets roll;
　Beyond the stars and central sun,
　Beyond where blazing comets run.
Where mind is lost in whirling space,
It doth its golden pathway trace
　To the throne of the Infinite; where
　It soars in bliss, and bows in prayer.
Its magic touch builds brighter domes
Than greatness, or the greed that roams
　For gold.　Ambition's lofty pride,
　Bold, Cæsar-like may sternly stride
Across the rubicon of love.
And spurn its joys.　May look above
　Its trampled bliss, and march ahead
　On steeds with bridles dripping red,
Till on a pyramid of bones
A throne is made of all the thrones.
　But on that dizzy sceptered hight
　The heart will shrivel with the blight

Of desolation, drear and dark,
Be sorrow's tomb, and envy's mark.

Love doth the fairest castles build,
Affection's gems doth deck and guild
    Its portals.   There fancy's wing
    Oft soars for new-found joys to bring
Into its temple.   The mind is but
Its messenger to ope and shut
    The door of reason.   The hands that toil
    The feet that swiftly tread the soil
Obey its bidding.   Memory holds
Her treasured stores to glad unfold
    Their fairness, and to fondly bless
    Its idols with a sweet caress.
Intelligence—that electric fire,
Is but the lightning 'long the wire
    Of its embodied hopes.   The heart
    Is but the battery whence they start.

She is the fair enchantress of the earth,
Whose wizard touch gives joy to birth,
    The sun-light, star-light of the soul,
    The monarch of the tides that roll
    From beings' center to its pole,
The pivot turning night to day
Heaven smiling on the darkest way,
    The essence of all warmth and light;
    While *hatred* is the gloom of night.

The chaos of an unborn earth
Till love hath spoke it into birth.
  The deluge that hath drowned the world
  In blood, nor built an ark.   But hurled
On life and time a thousand woes,
The curse of strife and death's repose.

Love doth not seek to fly
To glittering hights where Fame sits high,
  And breaths her zephyrs of applause,
  And weaves her laurels.   Her cause
Though hope may seek fame's nectared bowl
Is not distinction. The yearnings of the soul
  Are deep and strong. Her joys doth loom
  The brightest 'mid affections bloom.
There the heart pantings and its sob,
Are stilled by joys fame oft doth rob
  Joys drowned 'mid clamorous strife :
  But all of life's not made of strife ;
Silence is strong.   Though tempests roll
There'll come a lull—a quiet to the soul.
  Then turned from fame and greed of hire
  'Twill feel affection's central fire,
Volcanic like, lift far above
The peerless monuments of love.
  Lift like an isle amid the sea,
  An eden where the soul may flee ;
The only eden earth can bring,
Where bliss can smile, and joy can sing.

There on **Love's azure hights are built**
Bright castle domes of gold and **gilt,**
  That glisten when **the** morn's begun—
  A sapphire blaze **at set of sun.**
Where georgeous tinted rain-bows **loom,**
And fairest flowers of beauty bloom.
  'Neath rosy morns and tranquil noons,
  'Neath mellow suns, and laughing moons.
Where angels come. Their wings of light,
Like diamonds **quivering** in the sight.
  And in its portals like a **queen,**
  Love sits enchantress of the scene.
Waves **her mild scepter and the while,**
Smiles care away **with but** a smile.

She rules, but with a golden chain,
No galling yoke brings grief or pain ;
  But music swells the arches high,
  And ripples through the starry **sky,**
And beings brighter than the light,
And angels come and go in flight,
From starry worlds, to starry hight ;
  And plant a ladder on earth's sod.
  In foot-prints where Redeemer trod.
  That reaching up doth rest on God.
Where sweet as harp of thousand strings,
The soul is music on bright wings.
  And treads that ladder to its hight,
  Which ends in endless perfect Light.

Love is God's master builder, who
Rears fairer fabrics than doth strew
  Ambitions plains. They may not rise
  To dizzy hights to dazzle eyes,—
But bask like fragrant summer isles
'Neath golden suns, where pleasure smiles
  'Mid flowers. Where enchanting seas
  Ripple with entrancing melodies,
Enrapturing to the listening ears,
As music of harmonious spheres.
  Where Syren songs are heard and sung,
  And rich ambrosial fruit is hung,
'Neath nectared vines, and blissful bowers
Of sweet existence strewn with flowers.
  The heaven of all the heavens above—
  The God of all the gods—*is Love*.

Then sad, " O sad the heart that hath
No earthly angel?" And that hath
  Not heard the melody of love
  In human voice. A music 'bove
All earthly—more charmingly divine
Than Syren's song, or Circe's wine.
  Than Amphion's lute, or Orphean lyre,
  Whose strings thrilled with Promethean fire:
Apollo's harp of beauty rare,
Strung with his threads of golden hair ;
  Or where Æolia's wind-swept band

Finds softer touch than human hand,—
The life of life, the soul of glee—
The essence of all melody.

It is the joy of all the past,
Life's first bright dream, bright to the last.
The light of Hope—the bliss to be ;
The fruit of that once tasted tree
Of Eden life's perennial joy,
That sin and death could not destroy ;
Whose sweetness in its faded bloom
Is still exhaustless through the gloom
Of centuries.   The sword of fire,
Flaming from Cherubim could not expire
Its sweets.   Its fragrance spread,
O'er all the earth, survives, though dead.

It is the light that makes the day,
In heaven—they need no other ray.
They have no sun like ours here,
Love *is* the sun that lights that sphere.
And in the heart where it doth dwell,
The bosom feels its glowing swell,
As if another Eden fair
Bloomed with perennial gladness there.

EDEN DELL,

OR

LOVE'S WANDERINGS.

True Love ne'er made our manhoods weak,
Though mailed knees might bow as meek
As childhood's prayer.   They'd rise more strong
Than Sampson when his locks were long.
To love is noble, God-like, wise,
Who loves not hath no starry skies,
No rainbow spanning storms that rise,
His nature's warped to strife and wrong.

A silence broken by the wings
Of thought new voiced. A touch that brings
The charm of feeling when it flings
        Its cadence on a trembling lyre.
A sunbeam straying through a dream
Where thoughts of beauty faintly gleam,
Like Shadows of the things that seem
        The kindling of immortal fire.

A music in the atmosphere ;
A sadness in the sun-light clear
Like beauty smiling through a tear,
        Love's magic and its mystery.
A heart that stayed, a fancy strayed,
A soft sigh falling from a maid
As fair as e'er the gods have made,
        And who shall know its history ?

A barque shall sail a stormy main,
A heart shall wander in its pain,
And turn to find its own again,
        Love is the highest bliss of heaven !
And yearning souls shall hear the wail
Of blasted hopes sigh through the gale,
And some shall win, and some shall fail,
        Upon this star long tempest driven.

EDEN DELL, OR LOVE'S WANDERINGS.

CANTO FIRST.

THE PARTING.

Soft in the mellow light of day,
A beauteous landscape stretched away,
To where a smiling Eden lay.
To where the fairest flowers of spring,
Upon the cooling zephyr's wing.
Their sweetest wealth of odors fling.
Where fragrant honeysuckles bend,
Their graceful heads, as if to blend,
In whispered prayer for foe or friend :
Or having drank the sun-light through,
And waiting for their cup of dew,
Would ask a blessing for the two.
The air was soft as summers breath,
Fresh from wild flowers upon the heath,
While dimly in the distance gray,
Stood vernal groves in Spring array,
Like silent guardians of the day.
And emerald meads shone far and near,
Where wild flowers bend o'er streamlets clear,

Like dreamers in another sphere.
The dying day had almost fled,
The sun now tipped his cap of red,
As if he bade ' good night ' and said,
" I've kissed my love the blushing West,
I make my bow, and bid you rest."

There, where the purple shadows blend,
And vine-clad arbors arch and bend,
With arms entwined, *two lovers* stand
And gaze afar on that fair land.
Their souls drink in the mellow light—
The gold from off the sun-set hight.
Nor dream they of a coming night
Of life or love ; for hope is bright,
And earth has brought its sweetest charm
When souls with love are fresh and warm.
They stood with brow uplifted there,
Kissed by the soft-lipped evening air.
They both were young ; and one was fair,
With coral lips and soft brown hair.
Her cheeks had caught the roses hue,
Her eyes returned the sky its blue,
Yet sparkled with a richer hue
Than do the diamonds of Peru.
There, tall and beautiful she stood,
More graceful than a nymph of wood,
Or chiseled marble ever could.

He gazed in her up-lifted face.
His soul drank deep its truth and grace.
He thought that blest with love alone,
And such a darling all his own,
He'd have a heaven here begun
More dear than aught beyond the sun.
She was so young, so fair, so pure—
He could not bear the thought endure,
That few of noble deeds he'd done,
So littie fame and fortune won,
He blushed to look upon the sun.
So undeserved of such a prize,
He'd toil for gold 'neath other skies,
And earn her by some sacrifice.
For since the world sets so much store
On houses, lands and glittering ore,
He'd have his portion.   She should know
For her he'd tread the wide world o'er.

He pressed her to his heart so true,
And gazing in her eyes of blue,
Said, " Ethel, dear! My sweet, my dove!
While days shall shine, and heavens above
Smile on us with a look of love ;
While suns shall set, and stars shall rise,
And earth be wrapt in vaulted skies;
And tides shall come, and tides go back.
And white moons wheel upon their track,

I'll love you: and when suns grow old,
And earth fades like a blazing scroll,
I still will claim that I am thine,
And fondly dream and wish thee mine.

" But Ethel, I must speed me soon
Where early, late and 'neath the noon,
By steady work and earnest toil,
Where suns tan brown, and red sands soil:
Must get me gold, a name must get—
And show through years I love thee yet.
'Twere far too tame for me to claim
A prize so 'bove my lot and name,
A prize so dear that heaven alone
For loss of such could scarce atone.
For God found Eden naught to man
'Till woman came, then changed his plan.
And then old Eden took away,
And left her in its place, they say
When years have flown I'll come again
With love as true, nor one heart stain,
And bring with me the treasured gold,
And warmly to my bosom fold,
With love that's tried, and better told,
The one more dear than life or gold.

"Ah! say you stay? I would 'twere so,
Nor pride of love should bid me go,

Did not brave Jacob true as truth
Serve for fair Rachel in his youth?
Served fourteen years and deemed them naught.
So fair the prize his service brought.
And Paris with a fearless hand,
Fled with fair Helen to his land,
And ten years 'round the walls of Troy
Did challenge fate with steadfast joy.
Why then not I, for one more true
Dare bravely wait, and nobly do?"

"Stay, stay!" She said, "you must not go;"
Her voice was sweetly soft and low,
And with emotion trembling shook
Like murmurs of a rippling brook.
And gently did the silence break,
Like moonbeams falling on a lake.
She paused as if the thought were pain,
And bowed her head, then spoke again:
"The stars fixed in the crescent blue,
That steady shine so mild and true,
The bright sun whirling through the day
That constant keeps his gold pathway,
The ocean surging night and noon
That lifts white hands unto the moon,
That bathes her pale face in the sea,
Are not more true than I to thee.

" But if it be thy firm desire,
I will repress love's ardent fire.
Yet in my heart as in an urn,
Its glowing fires shall constant burn
Till God shall speed thy glad return.
This only promise will I claim,
Behold yon star of heavenly flame!
I named it in bright dreams in youth
The orb of love, the world of truth.
The heaven where with the one I love
I'd tread the shores of bliss above.
Vow, whether near or whether far,
When e'er thou gazest on that star,
Thou'lt strive to make thy love as fair,
And keep it pure as childhood's prayer
When each from each are far away,
We'll hold communion through its ray.
When gazing there think thou of me,
My soul shall answer back to thee.
And if we live or die apart
No fate can keep us heart from heart."
Each lifted to the star the hand,
Love sealed the vow as thus they stand
Imprinting with a rosy thrill,
A joy nor time, nor years could still.

Beneath the stars that softly shine
Where tangled moonbeams dance and twine

In garden wreathed with crescent vine;
They tarry where dark shadows meet
And learn of love its bitter sweet.
Arm twined in arm, lip touched to lip,
At love's pure fount they sweetly sip.
Nor know they naught but love's deep bliss
Sealed by love's signet-seal—a kiss.
And dark eyes gaze in orbs of blue
Reflecting back a darker hue,
Within whose azure depths the deeps
Of love's bright sea reflected sleeps.
Where, with love's sweet beguilings lit,
Love's fairest dreams like shadows flit.
While pass the hours swift and fleet,
And time glides by with noiseless feet.

Ah, me! What matter how they flee
When love sips honey like the bee?
For life has many hours, you see,
But none so fair, and none so sweet
As those that pass where love-lips meet.
For love that is the sweetest sweet,
Strews fairest flowers beneath the feet;
And leads, with soft bewitching grace,
Of parted lips and smiling face,
The rosy hours in joyous chase.
But then, ah then! the parting's nigh,
And fondest hearts must breath a sigh.

And darker shades the evening cast,
As swiftest hours are speeding fast.
While love must bow to sorrow's spell,
And bitter speak the sad farewell.

Most bitter sweet indeed to some
Does love with its beguilings come.
When hearts their fondest hopes must crush.
And love her brightest dreams must hush.
And hand that should be pressed in hand,
Meet only in the bright dream-land.

They parted there beside the gate,
Nor doubted time nor questioned fate.
Their parting words they whisper low,
While gentle breezes softly blow
As if to catch the whispered flow.
The moon looked down serene and proud,
Then glided through a fleecy cloud.
Within the moon and star light clear,
Her cheeks bejeweled with a tear,
As angel of another sphere,
As Peri on the golden strand.
He saw her in her beauty stand.
Departing now, through shadows far
He saw her gaze upon a star.
Unto that star he kissed his hand,
And on the morrow left the land.

*　*　*　*　*　*　*　*

Thus vowed upon their parting day,
Fair Ethel Vane, and Truman Gray,
 In Eden Dell.
Thus parted fondly, but in pain,
To meet, ah! when to meet again?
 Farewell! farewell!
For the sea will sink and swell,
 And the earth turn like a wheel,
But no wizard eye can tell,
 What the future will reveal.

For the heart is like the sea,
 Never waveless, never still,
Changing in its grief or glee,
 To the breezes of the will.
As the moon walks o'er the night
 As the sun dispels the shade,
May thy love grow strong and bright,
 As the stars that never fade.

FOREWARNED, A PROPHECY

Far Westward where broad prairies lie
Fringed only by a circling sky;
Beneath a tent in breezes fine
Three travelers at their ease recline.
Near by, within the sun's bright rays,
Their steeds upon the green plain graze.
The golden day most loving blent
The blue of plain and firmament
While in the circling sheen of light
The tent 'rose like a speck of white.
'Mid rolling waves of verdant hue
Spread far as eagle's eye could view.

The travelers mused. The meal was past.
The day a dreamy languor cast
That seemed to fill the soul with ease
And bring again the dreams that please.
They mused in silence, long, profound.
Unbroken by a breath of sound,
And wandered o'er the flowery ways
Of hope and love in other days.

They still were young, and loved to feel
The thrill of youth like flash of steel
Ere use and rust hath dimmed its shine,
And marred the flame upon its shrine.
To feel the glow, the flash, the gleam
Of passion's fire, and love's bright dream,
Was but their nature; and they felt
Those fires that ardent natures melt,
Yet oft leave harder than before,
Like lava cooled on ocean's shore.
These were Earl Darring, Hugh McVeigh,
And our young hero, Truman Gray.

At length Earl Darring silence broke
And stroked his beard, as thus he spoke:
"How strange is fate! A wanderer grown,
No land or home I call my own.
In youth, I loved a maiden fair
Who smiled with such a winning air,
I worshiped like a saint in prayer.
Her sunny tresses waving hung,
Like threads of gold to breezes swung,—
Like gleams of light the stars among;
And banded 'round with argent sheen
The brow of snow that rose between—
And crowned her as with gold—a queen.
A Hebe in form, a nymph in grace,
With hazel eyes and faultless face.

"We pledged our love in early youth,
And thought nor time nor nothing ruth,
Could ever change or blast its truth.
But partings come. They came to me.
We parted 'neath our trysting tree.
I placed a white rose in her hair
And thought she never looked so fair.

"The shades of learning then I sought—
In college walls sought lore, and thought,
I often burned the midnight oil,—
Her love was my reward for toil.
Oft gazed upon her image fair,
Oft thought of white rose in her hair,
And drew fresh inspiration there.

"When years had flown, like birds on wing,
And hope sang like the birds in Spring,
I sought her. Hoped she still sought me,
And found her 'neath our trysting tree—
Another with her—who was he?
I *saw* him bending o'er her, stand
With peerless white rose in his hand.

"I *heard* him whisper words of love,
I heard her answer like a dove.
He placed the white rose in her hair—
I turned, the sight I could not bear.

"I sought her on another day
When sunset shed its golden ray.
And, pausing at the open door,
I saw three standing on the floor.
Two clasped their hands—one fair, one tall,
Some words—a prayer—and that was all.

"I saw a white rose in her hair,—
I turned and faced the sunset there,
Reflecting back as proud a glare.
It seemed its light did then expire,
And in my blood I caught its fire."

He raised his clenched hand, and now
He drew it strangely o'er his brow.
Then paused awhile, as if he spoke
Some inward words, then silence broke.
"I journey now to the setting sun,
Nor care how soon the race is run
'Till I pour back in its fiery flood
This burning, red-hot, bitter blood.

"For up and down the world I rove,
Within my heart a buried love;
A memory haunts where'er I go.
For so it is—how oft its so."

[*He sings.*]

"Then I'll sing a song of a maiden fair,
With a white rose twined in her braided hair,
Of a maiden so rare with a rose so fair
That she tangled my life in her braided hair.

"Three roses white shone pearly fair
In her golden braids of sunny hair.
One I placed there, *two* he placed there.
It was so strange it seemed unfair.

"Oh! sad is the heart where there is not prayer!
Oh! sad is the heart where there's dark despair!
Oh! sad is the heart when no angel fair
Rolls away the stone from the grave that's there!

"Some think it strange and foolish quite
That I cannot banish three roses white.
But I pinned my heart to a maiden bright
And she brought me noon, and she brought me night.'

Then silence brooded for a while,
'Till Hugh McVeigh, with bitter smile,
Rose grandly up, and towering stood
Vehement in each changeful mood,
And scanning first the distance dim,
Where grass-blue met the sky-blue rim,
Spoke thus with warmth each varying word,
With eloquence they felt, who heard:

"I too have loved, I know not why,
It is the strangest mystery.
She was so grand, so fair to see,
And yet she never smiled on me.
I often smiled, it did me good
To look upon her proudest mood.
Disdain and pride. Ah! that was her—
She was as proud as Lucifer.

"She was a dark-eyed, tall brunette,
With queenly form and hair of jet,
Dark, rolling eyes, with flash of fire,—
A voice enchanting as the lyre.
With head erect, and scornful mien,
And glowing face of olive sheen.
She stood a haughty Tarquin queen.
Why did I love her? I could not bear
The pride of her disdainful air.

" And yet I loved. Beneath the sky
I scarce can find the reason why.
But more, for her I'd dare to die;
I'd dare all things known on earth's sod.
I'd dare all but the throne of God.
Dare stand upon the brink of hell
Where Lucifer and angels fell,
And fill it full of orphan's tears.
And all the lives of coming years.

Snatch devil from his hell of fire
And lift him to the tallest spire
Upon the blazing dome of heaven,
Jehovah's will denied or given.

"Seize evening star when thus begun
And burn it in the setting sun;
Grasp sickly moon with face so pale
And melt her in the comet's tail;
Tie blood-red stars, one by one,
With strings of fire unto the sun,
And toss them in that shoreless sea,
The dread, unknown eternity.
Yet from the wreck would save one star
On which to dwell with her afar,
Nor for the rest would sigh or groan,
If I but knew she was my own."

"'Tis sad to see," young Truman said.
"Your passion blaze to hottest red."
"I know it well," McVeigh replied,
"But love that deep when scorned, denied,
Is bitter in its sullen pride.

"I would not harm the human race,
Nor mar with blood kind nature's face;
But when my thoughts are in this mood
They're bitter as the Dead Sea's flood.

I would not shed one orphan's tear,
If every tear was a diamond clear,
As bright as the sun in its proud career,
As rich as the isles where the diamonds lay,
As pure as the stars on the brow of day —
Nor drag an angel from its sphere,
Though through, beyond time's rolling year
I might claim all that sphere my own,
And dwell upon a sapphire throne.

" But I'd brush from grief its briny tear,
And I'd rather lift a meek soul here
From its shivering tenement of clay,
To the brightest dome in the realms of day.
I'd wipe the tears from orphan's eyes,
I'd calm the breast that deepest sighs,
I'd cheer the weary fainting soul,
Lift merit to its highest goal,
Would bless the world the all I could,
Enshrine my life in noblest good,
And were the power to me given
Would make this earth another heaven—
An Eden far more pure and fair
Than when the Serpent snared The Pair,
And cursed the earth with strife and care.

" Why did I love?   I'm not so wise,
Because she had such glorious eyes

That glowed like twin stars in the skies.
Because her face was fresh and fair,
Because she wore a queenly **air**;
Because her beauty was so rare.
I never mused or knelt in prayer,
But that I saw an angel there
That did her sweetest image wear.
Because the deer will snuff the air:
Because the birds and beasts will pair;
Because the dove will seek a mate;
Because, because, such things are fate:
And heaven decrees them from above,
And this is why I can but love.

'' My love I breathed not. She well knew
My heart was warm, **my love** was true.
She saw it in my bashful eyes,
My love-lit look and glad surprise;
But, wounded by disdain and pride,
I tried to hate, and left her side.
And I will track **the** round world **o'er,**
Nor look on her proud presence more,
While **waves rise** up, and skies **bend o'er.—**
While **worlds have suns and** seas have shore.
And yet her proud face haunts me still,
I hear her voice in the bubbling rill,—
I see her form in the shadows still,
Is love the growth of human will?

I know not, yet too well I know,
I laid it where the willows grow.
And yet its ghost will come unbid
To raise again Hope's coffin lid.
I cursed all love beneath the skies,
I scorned it as a thing despised :
I trod my heart beneath my feet,
Yet, like the trampled flowers. more sweet
Its essence rose and softly stole
In honeyed fragrance to my soul.
Stand off. thou wizard of unrest !
My soul's my own, wouldst thou contest.
And manacle its free born will?
I hate ! I hate !—but love her still.
I know not if her proud heart cares—
I know that mine a dead hope bears."

[He sings.]

"Then I'll sing a song of a maiden bold,
As fair as the sun with his shield of gold ;
As proud as the stars on the throne of night ;
As cold as the snows on the mountain hight,
For she buried the hopes that once did abide
'Neath Alpine glaciers of lofty pride.

"Then I'll build her a throne of coldest stone,
And I'll crown her brow with a frozen zone.
A scepter of ice her hand shall wield,
And a world of snow shall be her shield :

And I'll send her forth to the hell of fire,
To freeze its plains for her *own empire*."

" How very bitter," Young Truman said,
"You should warm your heart, and cool your head.
In your earnest soul you should aspire
To noblest thoughts, and a pure desire.
Your love, like crooked mountain stream,
Runs from extreme swift to extreme.
But truest love glides smooth and strong,
Like streams that journey far and long;
Like rivers full, with tall banks steep—
Flow silent, strong, flow clear and deep.
You each, I fear, misunderstood
Your loves, you are so hot of blood.
One coldly tarried much too long,
The other loved too wild and strong.
The *fair haired maid*, long left alone,
Thought you had cold and careless grown.

"The proud brunette, with queenly form,
Thought you should all your cohorts form,
And take her as a fort—by storm.
The frigid crust was but a shield,
To urge advance, and charge the field.
No fault of heart, it was her pride,
While you stood off, that bold denied
What was unsought.   You should advance
With bolder step and lifted lance,

As if you sought to win the prize,
And be the chiefest in her eyes.
For coldest hearts if touched aright,
With streams of joy oft bless the sight,
Like rock in desert smote by rod
Of Moses at command of God."

" How oft the heart that seems so cold
Has in its core and inner fold,
A wealth of tenderness untold :
And knows that tenderness so well,
It strives nor word, nor deed may tell :
But wraps itself with outer pride,
The richness of its wealth to hide.
For richest nuts have hardest shell,
And deepest seas have softest swell :
The deepest griefs none ever tell,
And truest loves breath low 'farewell.'

" I, too, love one most sweetly dear,
Whose smile a desert heart would cheer;
With mind all goodness, gentle, wise :
With soft brown hair and lovely eyes.
Such eyes ! The soul's unfathomed sea
Lights up their depths of constancy.
O ! Who can tell the depths that roll
Within the ocean of the soul,
The hights that rise, the thoughts that burn,
Within the heart as in an urn ?

This makes the soul-lit features glow,
And their immortal grandeur **show**.
This subtle power of thought and mind,
I prize above all **gems** I find.
Yet *she* is dowered with every grace
Of lovely form, and charming face.
From her—from **love**, with courage **bold**,
I've turned awhile to seek for **gold**.
And I'll believe her warm and true,
As the light that paints yon azure blue,
"Till the sky shall **shrink to a drop** of dew."

The others 'rose and prompt replied,
" Ere earth her circuit thrice shall ride,
That vaunting boast shall be denied :
And thou, with hand uplifted high,
Swear life's a cheat, and love's a lie.
So give the hand, we then may meet,
And time will prove love bitter-sweet.
We've laid this unction on our soul,
To love no more while ages roll,
For like Sir Knight of ancient lore,
We cannot love, but we adore."

*　*　*　*　*　*　*

The sun from his zenith of gold,
Looked down in his pride as he rolled ;
These words to the breezes were told,
And the tent on the prairie they fold.

CANTO THIRD.

FOUL PLAY BENEATH THE STARS.

Beyond Sierra's hights of snow,
Where mountains slope to plains below,
And valleys rich in precious ore,
Stretch onward to Pacific's shore:
Where crested waves reach far and wide,
And ocean rolls her briny tide,
And in her surge of foamy crown,
The moons rise up, and suns go down.
Where walled about with mountains high,
And arched above with bluest sky,
A world of fairest edens lie.
Within a gorge, or valley deep,
A mining town lay still in sleep.
The scattered houses rambling seem,
And crooked streets befringe the stream.

One lonely wanderer watched the gleam
Of moonlight on the silvery stream,
And saw it glow and ripple there,
Like glossy gleams of soft, brown hair:

Like glowing smile **of** maiden fair.
Above, the moon rode pale and proud,
And oft a vail of fleecy cloud
Her modest face would strive to hide,
As one would vail a blushing bride.
Perhaps it was an angel fair,
That sought to vail pale Luna there,
And hide from her pure modest sight,
Dark deeds of men 'neath shades of **night.**

Young Truman, long for gold had wrought;
Had hoarded much, for more he sought.
And yet he knew earth's greatest pain—
A strong man's toil for wealth and **gain.**
His mind that night was troubled deep;
So restless that he could not sleep.
He wandered forth to calm his thought,
To cool his brow, the stream he sought.
He said, " I was too proud of soul,
Too proud to taste the nectared bowl,
Until I showed by deeds **of** worth,
I merit fairest of the earth.
The noblest aim may be misconstrued,
The noblest eyes with tears bedewed ;
The noblest heart be proudly spurned ;
The warmest love be cold returned ;
And noblest soul in this life here,
Be soiled with dust and dimmed by tear."

Then o'er the stream he bended low,
Then lifted eyes to hights of snow,
Then peering through the heavens afar,
Gazed on the setting evening star.
This scarce had done, when like a lance
Two robbers from the night advance.
They strike him there—when unaware—
A gash is in his parted hair—
A gash is on his noble brow—
And Luna's beams kiss softly now
The red wound on his pallid brow.
O! love of gold!   O! love of gain!
The heavens bend down with a look of pain
To see you slay—to see your slain!

The Moon bent o'er with a sickly smile,
As a mother bends o'er a dying child.
The Stars shrank in their vault of blue.
And said, " We will not look at you.
You look too pale and ghastly white,
To lie on the earth in the cold moonlight.
Have you no one to bathe your brow,
To shield and warm and cheer you now?
No willing friend in that far land,
To close that wound with gentle hand ;
To wipe the gore from your dark hair,
And from your forehead ghastly fair ? "
And the sighing Wind that whispered by,

Returned the stars this kind reply :
" I've kissed him for his mother dear,
Brushed from his eye the starting tear,
And caught the accents of his prayer,
And borne them on the listening air ;
And from the cabin standing near,
I caught upon my willing ear,
The ring and clink of sounding gold,
Where robbers entered fierce and bold.
I'll try the conscious cowards sore,
I'll shriek and moan about the door,
And whisper to all passers by,
Foul play!' And stars you must reply,
Foul play!' from out your crystal sky."

The Mountains nodded their assent,
And said, " This spangled blue hath bent
For ages o'er our snowy crest,
And all these ages have been blest
For man.   God raised our towering land
From ocean chaos, and night's strand,
To cool the breezes with our snow,
To water verdant plains below ;
To give our veins of golden ore
To grasping man.   But scarce before
Beheld we such a dastard deed,
Such fiendish crime, and hellish greed.
Is *gold* a curse on land and main,

More dark than curse on jealous Cain ?
And earth must bleed at every pore,
And man bleed at his own heart core ?
We'll whisper to the silent night.
Go hide man from Creation's sight :
Nor let the gazing worlds sublime
View record of such damning crime."

The silent Night. unvoiced before,
Moaned like the waves on ocean's shore.
And dropped her sable curtains down,
To hide the moon and starry crown,
And sobbing for the sinless years,
Wept o'er the earth with dewy tears ;
And brooding o'er the voiceless gloom,
Like sorrow o'er the silent tomb,
She watched the lingering hours pass,
While every Hour sighed, "Alas !
Alas ! alas ! that we should pass
And crime mark every hour glass
Since time began.   Since man had birth
Such gory land-marks scar the earth.
Since Cain. the first born. madly slew
His brother, blood wets earth like dew.
And seen upon God's youngest star,
The world of man, by worlds afar,
A blow—a gash—a half closed eye,
A pale face staring at the sky :

"Some spots like drops of setting sun,
A crimson, curdling as it run,
A mouldering clod that smiled no more,
While Silence wrapt it o'er and o'er."

CANTO FOURTH.

RETRIBUTION, OR THE VIGILANTES.

In the early dawn of the breaking day
Some horsemen gathered and rode away.
They urge with steel each bounding steed,
And skim the vale with whirlwind speed.
Armed and equipped they sternly rode,
And scour and guard each mountain road.
For a friend up early had passed that way
And roused the vigilantes' sway.
The honest miners banded strong
For common good, to punish wrong.
For dire necessity they saw
For self-preservation—nature's law,
And this the bond of union made.
An iron hand that power swayed.

As the sun arose, they rode again,
From out the mountains to the plain.
Two others with them led along,
Hands tied, and neck in lasso thong.
These struggled oft and oft held back,
'Till tightning up the lasso's slack,

They felt its grip around the neck.
The gasping life-breath slowly check.
Then leaning back they slowly walk
With sullen scowl, and grumbling talk.
"Till at the foot of mountain, where
It sloping fringed the valley fair.
They paused beneath a clump of trees
That nodded gently to the breeze.
And stood upon a grassy knoll
That ended where two streamlets roll—
In full view of the town are seen
To wave above the valley green.

The captain orders. " Halt.   Alight.
Now, 'Squire. swear your jury right
You six upon the grass there sit :
Try if they hang, or you acquit."
The hardy miners quickly then
In front of jurors bring the men.
Then, ranged around upon the grass.
All sit as slow the prisoners pass.
The Squire, there Alcalde called,
With shoulders broad, and caput bald.
A man of nerve, a man of head,
With look of learning 'rose and said :
" Hold up your hands.   You solemn swear
The right to shield, the wrong to dare
And crime pursue ; nor criminals spare."

One prisoner then with dogged mien,
Said " Hold on. 'Squire ! You think I'm green.
But I've been tried before, and know
That's not the oath ; so Judge, go slow.
When I killed Tim at Devil's Run,
The lawyer said the oath begun.
According to evidence and law,
And justice balanced on a straw."
" Now hold your lip !" the Squire said,
" I am a lawyer born, and bred ;
But you will wag your careless tongue
Like one I've read of, till you're hung."

The stubborn prisoner then replied,
With taunting lip, and look of pride,
" I heard a lawyer once declare
His loud opponent's pride to spare,
' Your vocal powers you should increase ;
Rome once was saved by gabbling geese,
So let your vocal powers ring,
Know this for history proves the thing,
A horse's neigh once made a king.' "
The jolly miners laugh around.
And say the 'Squire a " brick " has found.
The 'Squire, versed in legal lore,
Thought he was ne'er so stumped before :
And that the sham of legal form
He could with pompous pride perform,

In "buis" like this be wonderous wise—
Be wisdom's chiefest in their eyes.

So sternly then he scratched his head,
And thus with kindling ire said :
" I've seen the cur bay at the moon,
I've seen the owl frown at the noon ;
I've seen the rill laugh at the main,
I've seen the monkey strut the plain
And mimic men of seven-pound brain ;
But ne'er before have seen a cuss
At his own funeral make a fuss."
" You never heard how Sampson threw
The temple down, and thousands slew.
He made a fuss.   Had he your jaw,
Instead of the one he once did draw
Of your dead sires, he would have slain
A thousand more upon that plain—
For you are the first with so much cheek
Since Baalam's creature ceased to speak."
" And you're another," the 'Squire replied,
" And first to make an ox's hide
Cover so much, since Dido tried
To make one cover a city wide."

Wise, like an owl, with look profound,
Each witness then he called around :
" Now, all you boys rise up and stand,

You solemn swear with lifted hand
You'll speak the truth at my comand."
The evidence was blunt and brief.
" These are the men—there's no relief,
We tracked them up; got part the gold—
They acted like offenders old.
Their boots fit in the robbers' track,
They first owned up, then took it back."

With plainest words the truth is spoke
And oft there passed, a careless joke.
Though very rude, they felt the need
Of a power to punish—a head to lead
'Gainst the tide of crime, and life preserve,
And the rules of order by force subserve.
No lawyer to plead, no judge to sway,
They waited not for the law's delay.
A criminal once within their grip
Soon felt his neck in the halter slip.
This is one extreme; there is another.—
'Tis years of delay, and a world of bother
With criminal costs, and endless hope
To a felon wretch that should " pull rope."

Ere ten short minutes the verdict read,
" The robbers are guilty.—hang till dead."
So the Captain spoke. " You men go
And over yon limb the lasso throw.

And lift these two from the ground below."
"I'll save you that.   I'll climb a tree,"
One robber said, with reckless glee.
"With a little help, you may climb a limb,"
The Captain said, with a mimic grim.

The prisoner said, "It's a hard thing
To dance when another pulls the string.
You blunder, Cap: but a blunder made
By an English Admiral, sent to Hade
The Turkish fleet, and kindly bade
Down-trodden Greece be free:
Such a blunder you've made with me.
The jury's right; we did the deed.
But the crows may on my carcass feed.
If I don't warn you to shun with care
The life I've led, the guilt I share.

In youth I spurned a mother's love,
And cursed her ere I turned to rove.
But the curse I cursed, has fallen on me,
And followed me o'er the land and sea.
With evil companions I've wandered far
From religions sun, and virtues star,
And roving, drinking and gambling wild,
Will make an imp of an innocent child.
I was meant for a parson, my mother said,
But from the thought I sullen fled.

For a comrade told me one day,
As truants we rambled the hours away.
' That I would find, if I would search.
The fools of the family were give to the church.' "

The other prisoner who long had stood
In silent, stern, indifferent mood,
As they o'er the limb the lasso throw.
Now sadly said in accents low,
" Farewell, Oh sun ! And all below.
Evil companions led me astray
From paths of virtue, religions ray,
To gods of gold, and idols of clay.
My first bad act was to lead astray
A sinless soul from virtue's way—
A trusting girl, thoughtless and lone,
But it wrecked her life and damned my own."

The word was given, two bodies hung
From a pendant limb, and quivering swung,
As a pendulum swings.   And two souls
Took up their journey to other goals.
Took their appeal to a higher court
That has here no reporter or report.
But in the day of final assize
The triers will know if they acted wise.
And there the triers and the tried.
May stand together, side by side :

And the facts appear both clear and nude,
To a higher court to be reviewed ;
Nor Justice blind, but Eye that saw,
Judge by a wise and perfect law.

So while the sun in brilliant scorn,
Moved on toward the middle of morn,
The horsemen mounting, rode away,
From work they'd done, to work of the day.
And as they go they gazing turn.
With eyes indifferent, and features stern—
To see the sun in anger burn.
To see the work their hands have done,—
Two bodies dangling in the sun.
Man's cruel, be he savage or sage,
Like a beast in lair, or beast in cage,
If you only rouse his anger and rage.
Man's cruel, you may say what you can,
And reason it well with a master hand,
Once in rage the tiger may spare,
The lion some pity and feeling share,
Where man will slaughter, rend and tear.

For force and wrong go hand in hand,—
Such justice man deals out to man.
Crime must be punished, but ah ! then
How sad the need to punish men.
Yet if thou pity can'st bestow,

Place it not on the criminal low,
But he that fell beneath his blow.
And though justice should be blind
In executing it, you'll find.
It must be cruel to be kind.

CANTO FIFTH.

Beyond Sierra's heights of snow
Where mountains slope to plains below;
Within the mining town there stood
A modest cabin, plain and rude,
Where, tossed with fever, racked with pain,
Severely wounded, but not slain,
Where sunset, through the open door,
Shone softly on the cabin floor,
Upon his rude but tidy bed,
With pallid face, and bandaged head,
Lay Truman Gray.   For days had lain
Unconscious half of thought or pain.
The evening breezes fanned his brow,
His thoughts came stronger, clearer now.
He knew he stood beside the stream,
Yet since knew naught but as a dream;
But turning on his pillow now
He felt a soft hand on his brow.

He looked and saw two glorious eyes
Gaze on him with a glad surprise.

A dark-eyed beauty, fair of face,
Of Spanish or Castilian race.
A truer type, he ne'er had seen,
Of full, round form and graceful mien.
A mouth like pearls in rubies set,
Dark, dreamy eyes, with fringe of jet.
That drooped above their half-veiled light,
As dark clouds fringe the sunset hight.
Rejoiced to see the danger past,
And signs of life returning fast,
She bathed his brow, with tender mien,
And smiled upon him like a queen.

How pleased he was to see her near,
How sweet her voice seemed to his ear,
As thus she said: "Now, Señor, rest,
Thy fevers past, thy wounds are dressed.
I heard thy need of nursing rare
And thought a woman's tender care
Might save thee. So I came alone,
And watched beside thee all unknown.
So rest thee well, and thou shalt see
The one so loved, yet far from thee,
For whom thou in thy fever raved
And prayed to see—for thou art saved."

These words came, like a potent charm,
His hopes to cheer, his fears disarm.

His weary eyes then softly close
In nature's calm and sweet repose.
For on his spirit, soothing fell,
The tender touch of woman's spell.
The sympathy, the care and thought
Of woman's tenderness, had brought
Unto his spirit peace and rest—
As heavenly visions cheer the breast.

O! woman! with thy gentle care,
O! earthly angel, pure and fair!
O! heavenly guide to faith and prayer!
What were the earth, did not thy hand
Strew flowers in a desert land?
What were the sick bed, did'st not thou
Lay thy soft hand upon the brow,
And calm the pain and anguish there
By thoughtful sympathy and care?
And what were man without thee here,
Unblessed with sympathetic tear,
Unpolished by thy gentle grace,
Uncheered by thy bewitching face?
A savage rude, of culture void,
With soul debased and love destroyed.
A day without a ray of light.
A night without a star in sight.

The storms that doth the tall oak rend
But makes the supple willow bend.

So man, prostrate in pain or grief,
Finds in frail woman sweet relief,
Who feels the grief to others known,
More keenly than she does her own.
O bless the hand that tends the sick !
O bless the love that's warm and quick!
O bless the heart that's kind and true!
And sheds its blessings like the dew.
Then, woman you will fondly bless,
And vow to never love her less.
These thoughts came with the shadows deep,
Ere closed his eyes in balmy sleep.

As days passed by, she often came,
With smile of sympathy the same.
She bathed his wound and dressed it oft,
And spoke with voice so kind and soft,
It cheered him in his pain and grief,
And made his sickness seem so brief,
He almost wished the constant care
Of maid so lovely, kind and fair.

When months had rolled into a year,
And mountains bathed in sunlight clear,
In lofty grandeur did appear:
He bade adieu to land of gold,
And turned him to his love of old.
Among the few he bade adieu,

Juanita came, his nurse so true.
Her dark-eyed splendor was a sight
That none could see without delight.
And Truman saw, with sweet surprise,
A sadness nestle in her eyes,
And from her lips he heard a moan,—
He stooped to press them to his own ;
Thought then of loved ones far away,
And said, "We bid adieu to-day.
As wanderers on a rugged shore,
We've met. Henceforth will meet no more.

"As ships that pass upon the sea
And hold sweet converse as they flee
Across the main, then part with pain,
We've met, and ne'er may meet again.
We all are ships upon life's sea,
Bound for one port, Eternity.
Then let us part and gladly sail,
Like boatmen o'er the Shallops trail.
Not like those ships we meet at sea,
That dancing on, 'mid foam and glee,
Approach with canvas spreading white,
And glistening in the bright sunlight,
But turn to shadow when they're past,—
No sunlight on their hull or mast.
Like false friends, fair before our face,
Advancing with a smiling grace

And cordial mien, but turning black
As shadows when we turn our back.
I give thee as I now depart,
The homage of a grateful heart.
Where e'er it swells on land or tide,
"Twill turn to thee with grateful pride."

Juanita said, " This world to me
Seems brighter since I looked on thee.
Now, that I'll see thy face no more
"Twill seem more dark than e'er before.
The things we've nursed and watched with care.
Grow on our thought, and in our prayer.
I never nursed a pet or flower.
But what 'twas dearer from that hour."
They press the hand, and there they part.
She turned to still her aching heart.

She turned, and as she turned she met
Two jealous eyes of glossy jet.
Her Spanish lover drawing nigh
With dangerous glitter in his eye.
A scornful curve upon his lip,
A headlong torrent in his step.

" Fi! Senorita, lost your heart ?
You keep a trist that's hard to part.
What, tears within those lovely eyes ?

That fair-faced stranger shun, despise."
" Ah! Came you here to watch and spy ?"
" Nay, to upbraid, perhaps to die."
" What mean you ? 'Tis a strange reply ?"
" You soon shall know, for life to me,
Is worthless without love and thee."
" What, are you mad ? " Yes," and he laid
His hand upon her arm and stayed
Her step, a lurking devil in his look,
While passion all his being shook.

" Juanita Amiga, mad and wild :
For I have loved you since a child,
Since we as children gleeful played,
At keeping house, beneath the shade
Of those old maples, grand and hoar
That stood before your father's door.
My love's grown strong and wild,
But thine has vanished with a strange decline,
This must not be, my all, my life
Hangs on the answer, be my wife ?"

" Pedro Desoto ! Go thy way,
Or else beware, thou'lt rue this day."
" Thou knowest thy parents urge my cause,
Thou should'st be mine by heaven's laws.
Mine, only mine, else love will be
Through life a curse, a hell to me.
Thou wilt say yes ?" " I answer no,

'Tis worse than rude to urge me so."
"'Tis love or life.   Is this your will,
And this your stubborn answer still ?"
His hand then clutched his dagger hilt.
" If you persist, blood must be spilt."
" You've had my friendship till this hour.
Now. I defy, though in your power."

" Your doom is sealed by that reply.
You must be mine, or both must die.
Say that you will now where you stand.
Nor other man shall claim your hand.
Or blood shall flow where joy should beam,
And mingle in one common stream.
Our ghosts shall shriek to worlds below
Ere others press that breast of snow.
I'd rather tread the world of gloom,
A murderer's soul—without a tomb,
Than bear the torture I've endured.
Or lose the love my soul hath lured.
There's danger in my Spanish blood.
Who e'er before its anger stood ?"

He threw one arm around her waist
As if he sought but love's embrace,
She struggled, and could scarcely speak.
" Release me." with a sudden shriek.
When quick his dagger rose on high.
Its gleam flashed on the evening sky.

One moment more he'd sheathed the blade
In the warm bosom of the maid.
A hand behind, the weapon caught,
And turned it from the heart it sought.
Quick wrenched it from his grasp away—
Far on the heath the weapon lay.

He turned like bearded lion then,
" You seek to stay my vengeance, when
Was vengeance stayed from hand like mine?
Her doom is sealed.   I might add thine."
Then from his breast a pistol drew,
And quick as thought he aimed it too.
A loud report, the welkins swell,
As staggering back, Juanita fell.

While sharply spoke young Truman Gray,
" Desist! Thy murderous weapon stay."
Quick, Pedro, then to his own breast
The pistol placed—the trigger pressed.
Another loud sound smote the air ;
Then with a pang of mad despair
There, falling at her feet, he lay,
Soon food for earth and death's decay

Quick, Truman raised the fallen maid
Who silent as in death, was laid.
The trickling blood oozed from her side,
He gently ope'd her bosom wide,

And pressing back the robes of white
Beheld a sad and lovely sight.
Upon that swelling sheen was wed
The marble white with gory red.
He searched the wound with anxious grief,
Until he found, with glad relief,
The ball had glanced from its true course.
In distant air had spent its force.

Had grazed her throbbing breast of snow
And stained it with the crimson flow,
Of liquid life, but sparsely shed—
Kind fate thus snatched her from the dead.
He staunched the wound, and fanned her brow,
And bound her breast with 'kerchief now;
And sought with thoughtful words and kind,
To calm the current of her mind.
Her face was pale, her lustrous eye
Glanced at the scene, then to the sky,
While thoughts upon her spirit fell
That few can read and none can tell.

Now turn they where Don Pedro lay,
And saw life's ebbing tide decay.
He pressed his heart—he tried to rise,
Then looking up, he met their eyes.
And startled, with a wild surprise.
And 'mid his dying groans, he said,
As fast the ebbing life-tide fled,

" Forgive, Juanita! dear, farewell !—
I thought not in this frenzied spell
That love would work the deeds of hell.
O ! could I live to wipe this shame,
From out my life, from off my name,
I'd bear all pangs of grief or pain,
Nor at the darkest fate complain.
Could heaven reverse decree's of fate,
It ne'er had been too late ! too late !
The hot blood of my treacherous race
Hath often wrought such dark disgrace."

His head then fell upon the plain,
And he was past all earthly pain.
Juanita bends above him now
And wipes the death dew from his brow ;
And said, " I might have loved, not blamed,
Hadst thou been mild, thy heart more tamed.
But who would live upon a brink
Where passion's earthquake soon might sink
Their little world, its peace, its bliss,
In such a fearful wreck as this.
I might have loved him when a child,
His passion seemed romantic, wild,
But older years taught me to blame
His jealous heart, too fierce to tame.

" Another dream of life is o'er
And I have learned one lesson more,

My childhood friend, with whom I played
In childhood 'neath my home-tree shade,
Hath sought my life with vengeful steel,
And felt the blow he meant to deal.
Ah! Who can tell, what prophet know
Who, Brutus like, may strike the blow,
A well loved friend turned secret foe?
Who knows but fate may make its thrust
By hands we've loved to bless and trust,
And we in some assassin trace,
The lines of a familiar face?
My childhood lover, can it be,
Thus ends the chapter, jealously?

" Beware of jealous, mad'ning love,
'Tis not long-suffering, slow to reprove,
But like a hawk that rends a dove.
'Twould curse an angel in love's name
And burn it in hell's hottest flame,
Did it not yield to its desire
And quell the green-eyed monster's ire."

Truman, Juanita, now again
Part sadly with a deeper pain.
She thanked him for the blow he staid.
He answered he was more than paid,
By slight return fate thus decreed,
For her great kindness in his need.

*　　*　　*　　*　　*　　*　　*

Now evening cast her shadows pale,
And night drew down her sable veil.
But when the day dispersed the shade,
And came in robes of light arrayed,
Her parents rising, missed the maid.

CANTO SIXTH.

AMBUSHED—A SAD DISCOVERY.

Four times the sun from his bright hearth
Had warmed the circling face of earth.
Four times his dazzling course had rolled
Upon his wheels of burnished gold:
And day and night, and gloom and light,
Wheeled in their groves of endless flight.
Through winding vales where streamlets stray,
O'er hillsides, rocky, rough and gray
A stage coach slowly wound its way:
Amid Sierras Mountains far,
Ere they had known the palace car.
Ere locomotives' stirring tone.
Had waked those solitudes unknown,
And gliding o'er its path of steel
Caused vales to quake, and hills to reel.
With ribs of brass, and heart of fire,
And limbs that neither feel nor tire.
From throat of gloom and voice of steam
Shrieked its mad shrill unearthly scream.

Ere this fierce civilizer's tread,
Had waked the bison from his bed.

To rear his shaggy head and see
A monster wild and fleet as he.
Caused elk or antelope to skim
Less fleet, though of the swiftest limb,
The wooded vale or trackless plain,
And start to hear its voice again.
Ere savage waking from his dream
By trembling earth and fearful scream.
Had thought the spirits presence near,
And shuddered with a nameless fear :
As its proud tread, and echo fills
Unpeopled vales and silent hills :
And writes upon the earth that whirls
Mind is the umpire of the worlds ;
That tames the elements of wrath
And guides them o'er an iron path.

The stage rolled o'er the mountain road,
Rolled on for days with human load,
O'er valley, hill and rambling brook,
Through mountain gorge and shady nook.
When 'mid the woods in mountain glen,
A war cry broke the silence. Then
Deep volleyed thunder rolled so high
It made the startled eagle fly
From lofty perch on mountain high.
The echoes rolled the valleys through
And pealed unto the vault of blue.

In dark ambush the Indians lay
And shot into the stage that day.
Some dying fell within the stage,
Some in their sudden fear or rage
Sprang out amid the savage band
To find a bloody fate at hand.
Some strove with boldest courage then
And daring fought like desperate men.

What courage could avail them there,
Caught in a bloody savage snare?
Two struggling fell amid the rest,
One's head lay on the other's breast ;
And tresses fair, concealed before.
On Truman's breast lay red with gore.

And with fair face and palid brow
Looked on him almost dying now.
Strange accident!   And are they dead?
Hark ! List ! And hear what now is said.
While savages for booty led
Neglect to scalp the scattered dead.

" How sweet in death upon this breast
To lay the dying head to rest.
And when our spirits leave the clay,
Together mount to realms of day.
Our souls shall journey on in love
To perfect. endless bliss above."

"I could not bear, the parting there,
And so resolved all things to dare,
For love disguised his fate to share,
Unknown to track him everywhere.
I little thought so soon would close
Our journey to death's dread repose.
So soon would end love's bitter spell,
So soon we'd speak life's last farewell.

"But tyrant death we are thy slaves,
And mother earth must give us graves.
Dear mother earth that grim death mars
With little mounds—her battle scars.
But they who sleep like us unknown,
Rob death of monumental stone ;
For shafts that bear the dead one's name
Are but deaths monumental fame.

"But love is all, and life is less,
And time's a journey through distress,
While death's the gate to blessedness.
I'll gently kiss his forehead fair,
And part the ringlets of his hair,
A wound more ghastly now is there.
Perhaps in death my love he'll own,
And bless me with his dying groan."

These words smote on young Truman's ear
And on his cheek he felt a tear.

Returning sense now caught each word
And marveled much at what it heard.
He ope'd his eyes with vacant stare,
As one would gaze on viewless air :
And though disguised. he knew her there.

" Juanita. here! Great God!" he cried.
But when he ope'd his eyes to chide,
Her pleading eyes so well replied,
He only said, " Ah, me! Ah me !
Your life's to good to lose for me.
But love like oak and clinging vine
Together cling 'mid shade and shine.
Such is my love for one afar,
"Tis drawn like needle to the star.
And with such love as thine and mine,
I'd offer prayer at heaven's shrine.
There launch our souls that look above
On ocean bosom of His love
Whose name is Love.   By this best known—
By this adored before His throne."

While thus he spoke an Indian passed
Who heard. and angry glances cast.
Who came with features fierce and bold,
And robbed them of their gems and gold.
He seized Juanita's flowing hair,
A scalp so rare he could not spare.

He pierced its folds with keenest knife,
In her despair—receded life.
Quick, Truman, summoned all his might
And frenzied by the horrid sight,
Snatched from the Indian, where he knelt,
The hatchet dangling at his belt.
With sudden stroke he cleaved his brain
And stretched him with the others slain.

This effort caused fresh blood to flow,
His vision failed, his pulse grew low,
And conscious sense passed with the blow.
There, silent in that mountain vale
Lay lovers pallid, still and pale.
And spirits wandered in a clime
Unknown, and recking not of time.
One's head lay on the other's breast,
One smiled as if in peaceful rest,
And fancies wandered in the shade
Where spirits meet, and dreams are made.

Down in the glen the shadows grew
And twined in purple and rosy hue,
The sun stooped down, and did unfold
His banners bright of red and gold.
The dying day did slowly fade,
And nature assumed a sadder shade.
The woods bent o'er like an arching sky,
The evening breeze, like mourners sigh

Wailed through the lonely forest nigh.
And 'mid the twilight shadows gray
The roaming panther stalked for prey.
The whip-poor-will poured forth his strain.
The night-owl hooted his refrain.
And dismal in the distance dark
The prowling wolf sent forth his bark.
The lonely pines on mountain's brow,
And weird groves in the valley bow
Unto night's ghost of drowsy air.
Like patriarchs in silent prayer.

On nature's face shown dewy beads
Like tears just wept o'er cruel deeds.
While through the vale and woodland there
An Indian camp fire threw its glare,
And crimsoned with its tinge of red
The distant sky that hung o'er head.
And where the dismal embers glow
Grim dusky forms move to and fro.
And night with plumage of silence fell
O'er the lives of some in that mountain dell.
And draping the hills with her pall of gloom
She bent like a mourner over their tomb.

CANTO SEVENTH.

A RIVAL AND A FRAUD.

The day declined, and splendor fell
From golden hights o'er Eden Dell.
Glad nature robed in emerald gay
Smiled 'mid the early flowers of May.
The birds were warbling in their mirth
And gladsome was the verdant earth.

The beauteous day was almost past
The Sun his slanting arrows cast
And shot his golden lances bright
From out the gorgeous sunset hight,
As if he sought to drive away
Night's cohorts dark in black array,
That hovered o'er his glowing realm
As if with chaos to o'erwhelm.

As day declined, and shadows fell
O'er wood and wold, o'er hill and dell,
And spread and grew in the evening late,
Fair Ethel stood at the mansion gate;

And gazed to see the evening star
Rise in the crimson west afar.
"O star!" she said "with ray serene
That proudly looks, and smiles a queen—
The queen of love, bright Venus. thou.
That glows upon night's sable brow.
Like love a star that rules the night
And heralds forth the coming light.
That guides us through life's setting day
And guilds it with a gold pathway.
Well named, well fed with sunbright rays
So near the sun in sunbright blaze.
Like love a star of brightest sod,
One near the sun, one near to God."

She sighed " A year has slowly passed
Since on his form I looked my last.
Since standing here 'mid shadows gray
I said farewell to Truman Gray.
Sweet were the loving hopes he told
Ere parting for the land of gold.
O evening star, perhaps even now
He turns to thee uplifted brow
With sun-brown face and care-worn air
Looks on thee with a wistful prayer.

" But Beaumont comes with studied part
As if I dare withhold my heart.

Complacent boor, he seeks my love
As hawk would seek to mate a dove
Their lawful prey, he'd steal my wealth
For love of gold and love of self.
And burn me at a martyr's fire
When e'er his passion lost desire.
He cannot love, love is unknown
To him who loves himself alone.

" Ah wealth's too small a recompense,
For lack of honor, heart or sense.
To him that's absent I'll be true
While stars shall deck yon crescent blue
Or moons shed silvery light afar
O'er waves that leap to grasp a star."
A tear then dimmed her eye of blue
And sparkled like a drop of dew.

" Good eve Moiselle ! You muse and wait
As if a lover lingered late.
From my abode across the vale,
While sitting in the twilight pale
Like Abram in the evening cool
When rare exception not the rule
Two angels did before him pass ;
I spied you with my opera glass.
And as no angel passed my way
I thought I'd seek one, listen pray.

The gracious proffer that I made.
A richer jewel ne'er was laid.
At feet of woman.   Is it true.
Another answer is my due?
With weal or woe that answer's fraught,
A jewel for your wisest thought."

" Kind sir, you come from very far,
To see a maid gaze at yon star,
When you can pluck it from its sphere,
And lay it at my feet just here,
You may receive the wish you name,
"Till then my answer is the same,"
" Relentless one you do not mean ?"
" I mean it all, the golden sheen
Of yon bright star, shall be the guide.
To fix my hopes where they abide.
For there were many ages when
Stars fixed the destiny of men,"

" And there were times," he quick replied.
" When woman's fickleness or pride
Caused wars and slaughter, tears and blood.
Disrupting States that long had stood.
A Helen's faithless, truant mood
Caused Troy's fall, and for ten years
Broke round its walls a thousand spears."

Then she: "But woman's truth alone
Once hurled a Tarquin from his throne.
A Charlotte Corday in her wrath,
Deposed a tyrant at his bath."

"Yes, but a false Delilah made
A Sampson's strength to wane and fade;
And Clytemnestras' murderous hand
Slew, by dark fraud, that kingly man.
Pierced, at the joyous festal board,
The heart where she had reigned adored.
Nor cities unbesieged should boast
'Till they've repelled the assailing host.
Beauty 'gainst wisdom, that is thee;
Wisdom 'gainst beauty, that is me."

"You're wondrous wise, and fain would teach,
None can withstand your polished speech.
That question's tested, if you please,
Beauty out-plead wise Socrates."
"How so? ah! I remember, too,
The story's old and counted true
Fair Pryne and Socrates were brought,
Both for impiety they taught.
Before the Grecian judges, there
To plead for life—one wise, one fair.
The sage, he plead with wisdom rare;
Fair Pryne arose with modest air,
Unveiled her snowy bosom fair,

And answered naught.   From hence
Beauty was wisdom's eloquence.
The sage the deadly hemlock drank—
Fair Pryne the grateful judges thank.
'Thy gracious act and breast so fair.
White-bosomed Pryne. thy life doth spare.'

"But fie! had one, not wise but bold,
Held in his hand some shining gold,
Each judge's itching palm would say.
'Not guilty. go thy honest way!"
Then. where is beauty—wisdom?   See
The gold is strongest of the three."
"Is that your fortress? Know this, then,
I choose a man from noblest men,
And gold is oft the crust, to hide
The rubbish 'neath its polished pride.
For oft true "gold o'er dusted's" passed,
For "dust o'er gilded," till at last,
The fraud's discovered and you scan,
'Tis principle that makes the man."

"You are sagacious at a hit,
Who edged the diamond of your wit?"
"Not thine. but Beaumont in my mood.
I seek not angry converse rude.
I'd rather dwell on memories past.
Than rainbow hopes the future cast.

They fade like bubbles on the main,
But joys once tasted still remain,
Like buried friends their image cheer,
With face as bright and eye as clear,
Within our souls, though their fair grace,
The busy worms long since did taste.
Naught can endure like joys of soul,
All else fade like a blazing scroll.

" The mind, the soul immortal wings,
Its flight above material things.
What men call matter firm we find,
Endures not like the viewless mind."
Then Beaumont spoke, " I've news that's strange,
Yet o'er my hopes it brings a change ;
It is a letter from a friend,
That says thy lover met his end
By robber hands upon the brink,
Of stream where he had stooped to drink.

"A stream that glided near his door,
They found him weltering in his gore.'
A shriek then rent the evening air,
Two hands were lifted as in prayer,
And Ethel reeling, fainted there.
She would have fall'n, but in alarm,
Quick Beaumont stayed her with his arm.

"O God!" she said with sobbing moan.
"It cannot be, to thee is known,
If in the far wilds of the west,
The clods lie o'er his pulseless breast.
O death thou art a shadow here,
A spectre ever following near;
Where ere we turn with sudden glare,
Thy hollow eyes upon us stare.
Thou sits a guest at every board.
Grins with the miser o'er his hoard;
Entwines thy arm around the strong,
Nor youth nor strength availeth long.

"O! life would be a sweeter dream.
Did it not end in death's cold stream.
Did we not hear the dismal roar.
Of death's cold waters at our door;
And know no light nor cheering gleam,
Shines o'er this dark Plutonian stream.
That those who've crossed this Stygian shore,
In all the ages gone before:
In all the many crossings o'er,
Returning, cross it *never more*.
O death in life! O life in death!
The slow pulsations of the breath,
Are but life's slowly dying death.
For we consume the things which seem.
To give us life, and thus we dream,

That we are living, breath survives,
But we are dying all our lives.
But Oh! that human blood should pour,
And human hands be dyed with gore."

Then Beaumont, filled with anxious fears,
Lest his rude message brought more tears,
Bethought him he would be discreet,
Lay his condolence at her feet,
And tender what to her would be
Or seem, the truest sympathy.
And thus he spoke, "O dearest dear,
My heart's best idol and its cheer,
Pardon my words that broke your peace,
Pardon my selfish joys increase,
That death should thus your vows release.
It wounds my heart to see thy grief,
Thy form shake like an aspen leaf,
Thy velvet cheek and soft eye clear,
Now crystaled by grief's briny tear.

"True, but for death, life would seem bright,
And earth scarce have a starless night.
We ne'er would stand beside the bier,
And seldom see a falling tear.
No cities of the silent dead,
With sculptured shaft above each head.
No kiss to bloodless lips compressed,
No pale brow that death hath pressed.

Then life would be a glorious dream,
And earthly joys more what they seem,
Then men would learn each foot of soil,
For what, and how, and when to toil,
Science and learning then would rule,
Earth be one fam'ly, not an orphan school,
While from the marts and vales of earth,
Would rise the joyous notes of mirth.
But such it is not; and the why?
'Tis written, 'man shall surely die.'

" Yes, man must fade like Autumn leaf,
Be garnered like the Autumn sheaf,
Until the great and final day,
When earth and sky shall pass away,
Even rock-ribbed earth shall crumbling melt,
The firmament be cracked and rent,
The moon shall cease to shed her light,
The stars to deck the vault of night,
The sun plunge from his golden sphere,
And darkling close his bright career.
Then grieve not, Earth with all its joy
Hath not one bliss without alloy :
Hath not one hope it may not blast,
Hath not a joy that's doomed to last.

And though we grieve from morn till eve,
And constant sighs our bosoms heave

From eve till morn, from day to day,
Until we grieve our lives away;
What boots it but a mind distressed,
A feverish brow, and sad unrest?
Then cheer up, fair and cherished friend,
On God and truth and heaven depend."
She weeping spoke, " Your words are kind,
While mine were rude and unrefined.
Such words of sympathy are rare,
I should have judged your cause more fair."

Then gently leaning on his arm,
With sense of sympathetic charm,
They strolled up to the mansion door
Where spoken farewells soon were o'er.
The closed door shut her from his sight,
Then Beaumont strode into the night,
And walking swiftly, shook his head,
As darkly to himself he said :
" I trust he's dead, how false was I,
My friend wrote he would likely die.
But this I vow with sullen brow,
And strength of will that naught shall bow,
That I will make her think him dead—
Me, and no other, shall she wed."

CANTO EIGHTH.

THE CAPTIVES.

Amid Sierra's Mountain wilds,
Where earth lifts up her hugest piles,
In snow-capped grandeur hoar and proud,
Up through the ether to the cloud,
Upon whose breast of snowy crown
The angels stop in coming down,
And spirits heavenward pause to rest
Upon its tranquil snow-white breast—
At least it seems it must be so—
A stepping stone to worlds below,
A place to plume the wing of flight,
Up through the vast empyrean hight,
Toward the golden mansions bright,
From which to leap and vault afar
On to some bright and glowing star.

And having journey thus begun
Sweep onward to the central sun :
Sweep upward till the wings are bent
O'er heaven's eternal battlement.

Far westward through these mountain wilds,
Far northward through their dark defiles,
Now upward on the mountain side,
Now downward through the valley wide.
A warrior waved his battle brand
And led a fierce and savage band.
Whose sable plumes in knotted hair
Waved to the breezes and the air.
Like crimson clouds at sunset low,
The war paint on their faces glow.
They had within their dismal train
Two captives wounded, almost slain.
And one was fair, with raven hair,
And one was sad with dark despair,
One sought to ease the other's care.
Oft smiled on him with hopeful air,
Oft lifted eyes as if in prayer.

The early morn was crisp and cold,
The sun now rose with shield of gold
And kindly warmed with genial ray.
The ether fields of glowing day
They'd journey'd long, and journey'd far,
And now seemed demons from a war.
Who led in fierce and dismal gloom,
Two captives to a horrid doom—
To burn them in a fiery tomb,
Or hurl them down a gulf of gloom.

LOVE'S WANDERINGS.

Through forest path and woodland wild,
Where forests greet her forest child:
They journey forward, journey on,
While suns rise up, and suns go down.

At length, toward a day's decline
They pause in grim and serried line
Upon a rough and rocky ledge
That jutted o'er a mountain's edge,
And saw the blood-red sun descend,
Where sky and ocean seemed to blend—
A monarch wrapt in scarlet gown
That parting doffed his dazzling crown.
The chieftain then his falchion waves,
And turning, thus addressed his braves:
" Warriors, our journey soon will close
From toil and march we'll take repose.
Far yonder on the mountain hight,
That's dimly outlined to the sight,
Upon the morrow, face to face,
Meet sachems of our ancient race,
To counsel how our wrongs to ease,
And the Great Spirit to appease.

" The mighty spirit high in air,
To whom the red-man lifts his prayer,
Who sends the bison and the bear;

Whose voice is in the thunder's roar,
His foot-prints on the pathless shore ;
His eyes shine from the glittering stars,
Earth 'neath his footsteps trembling jars.
His smile glows in the silent moon
And lights the dazzling **sun at noon.**

" Yon sun that now 'neath ocean's flood,
Seems wrapt and veiled and bathed with blood,
'Tis omen red that blood be shed,
To turn his vengeance from our head.
A human victim then must bleed,
To-morrow we'll supply the need.
The pale-faced captives, now our prize,
Shall be the proffered sacrifice.
Their smoking blood propitious rise
Up through the ether to the skies.
Their ashes from the altar place
Be blown into the sun's bright face."
A moment stood they silent there,
A yell then rent the startled air,
That seemed the very earth to fill,
And make the trembling sky to thrill.
'Twas answered from a distant hill.

And there they camped. While twilight gray
Stalked o'er the fields of parting day.
The night came down in mists of gloom,
The distant mountains darkly loom.

The captives weary, pale and weak,
Dejected sigh, but do not speak.
They hear the roaming panthers cry,
The wandering night-owl passing by ;
The distant coyotes dismal bark,
And night seemed drear, and hope seemed dark.
The yellow stars came one by one,
From out the sky so dark and dun ;
Like beams of light from angels' eyes,
Or new-born hopes dropped from the skies.

At length the moon rose slow and pale,
And pierced the gloom on hill and vale ;
And then rode on serene and grand,
As guiding to the " better land ; "
As pointing with a look of love,
To fairer worlds that smile above ;
To distant stars and central suns,
Where God hath housed his better ones.

The mountains leaned against the clouds,
And wrapped in snow, seemed in their shrouds.
That band of pearls and silver spray,
Heaven's jeweled arch, the milky way,
Seemed as a wreath upon night's crown,
Where angels stand in looking down ;
There view earth's troubled scenes of Time.
With sad compassion, love sublime.

From out the night a spectral shade,
Shown o'er the youth and captive maid;
And vast and shapeless gloomy stands,
Obscuring heaven with bony hands;
While through its ribs like dungeon bars,
They dimly saw the ghastly stars.
It stood a grimly, giant form.
Enwrapt in mists of gloom and storm ;
And towered through the vast expanse,
With scowling brow, and cynic glance.

While o'er them bowed its gastly face.
That seemed to come and go through space ;
And beckoning with its bony hand.
It pointed down night's sable strand.
While thus they gaze they dimly saw,
Upon the hights the angels draw,
Their noiseless bows.   The arrows flew
And pierced the horrid monster through ;
But still he rose more tall and grand,
And fiercer waved his bony hand.

The captives tremble ; but we see.
That shadow is dark Destiny ;
Outlining on the future's scroll,
The tests of time that try the soul ;
While from the heavens the angels view,
O'er shadowing evil grasp the true.

And rear her grim distorted form,
To take the soul by stealth or storm.
While through each dark and fateful night,
They shoot their arrows tipped with light:
And bid the hopes that never set,
On Star-crowned wings to linger yet.

CANTO NINTH.

HIDDEN VALLEY, AT THE STAKE.

Far beyond the West and Northland,
Far beyond the plains and Mooreland :
Where majestic mountains tower,
In their grandeur and their power.
Where the hills rise rough and rocky,
And the vales are deep and sombre ;
Stands a grand and rugged mountain.
On whose side flows forth a fountain.
Near a rock that beetles over,
Like a shelter and a cover,
To a cañon far below it.

Could you see it, could you know it,
You would say that mountain never,
Rose so grandly to dissever,
The fair vale and the blue ether.
Fair this scene amid the mountain,
Fair, the bright and sparkling fountain.
Hid amid the hills and woodland ;
With no eye to view its brightness,

And no lip to taste its waters,
As it bubbles in its laughter :
At the weird and wild scenes blending,
With the solemn sky o'er bending.

In that cañon calmly lying,
Walled by cliffs, all storm defying :
Lay a lake beneath the mountain,
'Neath the rocks, fed by the fountain :
Still and tranquil as the morning,
Calm as lips well skilled in scorning,
Clear as souls all guile disproving,—
Cold as hearts unloved—unloving.
Like the eye of Faith fixed riven,
Gazing up alone to heaven :
With the cliffs like hopes around it,
Reaching high but not to bound it.

Reaching high, and reaching higher,
Like some grand cathedral spire,
Whispering to the clouds above it :
Heaven is fair and I will love it.
In the night the stars are shining,
Crimson suns at day's declining,
Gild the clouds with silver lining.
We can gaze without repining,
Far upon earth's bosom lying
Only *human hearts* are sighing.

Thus the lake within the cañon,
Thus the mountains wild and rugged,
Thus the waters looked to heaven,
Pure as faith, cold, fixed and riven;
Thus the eagle of the northland,
Gazed upon the Hidden Valley;
Soared and flapped his wings with pleasure,
Perched upon some pine or cedar,
Then arose, and in wild laughter
Called his mate that followed after.
Dipped his plumage in the water,
Soared from cliff to cliff still higher.
Sought the sun, till nigher, nigher—
They were specks amid its fire.

Farther down this cañon widened,
Miles below it spread and widened,
To a valley rich and charming,
Filled with game unharmed—unharming.
On whose breast, 'tis fair to see it,
Shines a lake that nestles in it.
Shines another lake and glistens
Like a diamond in its casket,
Like a brilliant set in emerald;
Sparkling like a dew-gemed blossom,
Or a pearl on woman's bosom.

For the lake was as a mirror,
Glossy with the sunshine on it,

And bright landscapes dancing in it,
With white pebbles on its margin,
And the golden sands that glisten,
While the wild deer pause and listen
As they drink its placid waters,
And the bubbling streamlets laughter,
As it ripples o'er the pebbles,
Adds its new supplies to brighten,
And its dancing surface whiten
With its melted snows from mountain,
And its bubbling like a fountain.

With bright verdure spread around it,
And the mountain sides to bound it,
What can break its charm or sever
Its wild music and its beauty ?
'Tis a savage band with booty,
With sad captives sitting dreary,
As lone trees upon the prairie,
By the storm king torn, disheveled,
Shattered, branchless, and dismantled.

Or like pines upon the mountain,
Shivered by the lurid lightning :
When the wailing winds keep sighing,
And the dismal rain is sobbing :
And the tempests' roar is roaring,
And the plunging torrents pouring.

Some are sad, and some are lonely,
Some scenes wild and rugged only,
Some hearts full of melancholy,
Grieving o'er some hopeless folly,
Grieving over riches vanished,
Or some hope that time hath banished.
Brooding o'er some bitter sorrow,
Dreading clouds and storms to-morrow.
Hearts in gloom and sack-cloth dreary,
Sighing sadly, "I am weary.
Bright shall be my hearth-stone never,
For my loved are gone forever."
These are weary, but more weary
Are lone captives sitting dreary,
Bound and waiting, only waiting,
Powerless in their love or hating.
With the future spread before them
Like a bleak and stormy ocean,
With no eye to seek and love them,
But the storm-clouds bent above them.

On the rock with sides so rugged,
Beetling o'er the mountain jagged,
Near the trees so lone and cragged,
With the heavens far above them,
And the cañon far beneath them,
Sat a band of Indian warriors,
Brooding o'er their ills and sorrows.

Dark and silent, stern and savage,
Dreaming peaceful lands to ravish,
With their fierce red demon faces,
Savage as the tiger races,
With their wampum belts around them,
And their dangling scalps about them.

" Bring the captives, we will burn them,
We will torture, roast and turn them."
Said a stern and gloomy chieftain,
Who seemed chiefest and seemed spokesman.
"They shall scorch and shrink to charcoal,
'Till their ashes, scarce a handful,
Shall be blown o'er all the landscape,
That the pale-faced chiefs may tremble,
When the warriors red assemble,
Fly like eagles to their aeries,
Swift as whirl-winds on the prairies,
Nor their rifles scare the bison,
For these lands we did inherit,—
Thus we'll worship the Great Spirit."

The captives were brought, one manly one fair,
They trembled at naught, but smiled at despair :
The captives were brought, but 'twas sweet even there,
To behold how *she* sought to dispel his despair.

The captives were bound, on her wrists soft and fair,
The thongs were tied round with the rudest of care :

And then they were led to an altar of stone,
Where a fire burned bright 'neath a tree cragg'd and lone.

Then in soft Spanish tongue she said in firm tone,
" **For** this brave loved and young, let me die alone;
But save *him*, his life a ransom **will bring**,
He is god-like in strife, and great **as a king.**"

But " Nay," said the chiefs, "a lily to die,
Like a chieftain so brave? and a warrior to fly
From the terrors of death. like the timid of heart ;
Like the roe at the breath of the breezes to start.

" And tremble with fear ?   Fie! pallid of face!"
Then Truman spoke clear. with valor and grace :
" I fear not the death, but how cowardly thou,
If my hands thou'lt untie, I'll write ' Cain ' on thy brow,"

Then snapped his thongs with a wrench, snatched a torch
        from the trench,
In the face of the chiefs. its blazes doth quench ;
Then he sprang like a deer, with the torch in his hand,
To where, some steps in the rear. kegs of powder doth stand

In the rifts of the rock. with rifles near by.
With a bound and a knock, and the words. " All must die ;"
Quick. he lifted the brand. while all held their breath.
Then 'twas hurled from his hand. to the red flash of death.

Then *he* sprang from the rock, while there shot to the sky,
A red glare, with a shock, that resounded on high;
And the rocks and the cliffs, far to heavenward go;
To the height of the clouds, to be dropped far below.

While the loud thunders peal, 'till they shake the vast hill,
And the earth seems to reel, clouds the valley to fill;
And the rocks strew the vale, by the lake and the rill,
And the blue sky looks pale, ere the echoes grow still.

And the rock that had hung, beetling over the vale,
From its base had been swung, and now scattered the vale:
But where are the red chiefs, where the fair and the brave?
Do they soar on the cloud reefs, is the valley their grave?

CANTO TENTH.

THE AGED CHIEF.—A LEGEND.

Bright in the glowing east afar,
In argent sheen sank morning star ;
While fringed and draped with golden lace,
Aurora came with beaming face.
One day had passed, the next begun—
That glorious orb of day, the sun,
Came forth his proud career to run.
The valley smiled beneath his rays,
The mountains rose to greet the day ;
And lifted their uncovered head,
To praise the God who blessings shed.

The lake upon the valleys breast,
Like cups of silver lay at rest ;
Yet sparkled in the sun and air,
Like diamonds in a maiden's hair.
Like beautiful lake Como, when
She smiles amid her Alpine glen,
The mountains girt the beauteous vale
With battlements of emerald pale.

As fair a gem 'mid mountain sea.
As the far-famed vale of fair Tempe.

Toward the valley's farthest end.
Behold an aged savage bend
Upon his staff beside his cave.
He was an ancient chief and grave.
His head was bald, his locks were white.
His eyes were sunk and dim of sight.
His form was bent, his look was mild
And years had flown since he a child
Had wandered far o'er mountains wild.
The cave wherein he did abide
Was dark within the mountain side.
With trembling limbs he trod the vale.
With head all bare, and forehead pale.

There on the morn of that fair day,
In saddest plight 'rose Truman Gray.
Wounded and bruised and sick and sore.
Dejected by the griefs he bore.
For having leaped from mountain edge
And rolled adown its rocky ledge,
He scarcely had escaped with life—
Near ended thus his hopes and strife.
But landing on the brim of lake
Its spongy soil his fall did break.
He 'rose benumbed and weak with pain.
And wandered o'er the valley's plain.

With faltering steps along the **brake,**
He doth his **toilsome** journey **take.**
Till passing **up the valley higher**
He stands **beside the aged** sire.

"**Whose** step is this that wander's by?"
The **old man said** with startled cry.
"**A stranger,** wounded and distressed,
Who seeks for shelter, food and rest,"
Said Truman Gray, though scarcely each
Could understand **the other's speech.**
The aged said. "**My welcome guest**
Enter my cave, take food and rest."
He entered where **the aged dwelt,**
While grateful thanks **his bosom felt.**
And there abode he in that cave
The old chief's guest, to nurse **and** save.

While months pass on, and days fly by
Like **winds** that bear the wanderer's sigh.
They learned each others speech to know,
And strangeness turns to friendship's glow.
Together stroll they o'er the brake,
Together angle in the lake.
On game and **herbs and** mountain trout,
And springs that from the mountain spout,
They feast and drink ; till strength returns
To Truman Gray, whose bosom yearns,

And in his sweetest dreams doth start
To clasp the idol of his heart.
Then wakes to find her presence flown.
And he a distant wanderer lone.
The ancient sire his thoughts beguile.
And tells with weird and sober smile,
The tales of distant years and days.
Of hunts and wars and savage ways.
Of the quaint legends of his race.
Backward their lines of lineage trace.
When in their pristine strength and prime
They trod the banks of ancient time.
For never yet did any race
Backward its stream of lineage trace.
But what in wonder and amaze
They said ' What giants in those days.'
Though weak to greatest tribes have grown.
And greatest nations little known
How through the mists of time to trace
The ancient sires of their race.
Still standing o'er their mouldering clods,
They claim them off-springs of the gods.
One legend did our hero please
That told of ancient lands and seas.
Of noble braves of paler face.
The ancients of his ancient race.
In language thus the legend ran.
Thus slowly spoke the aged man.

THE LEGEND.*

Far across the world of waters,
     Far back in the time's fold,
In a land of vines and sunshine,
     Dwelt the pale-faced warriors bold.
In a land of templed cities,
     Walled about with stone and earth.
The Great Spirit was their father.
     He ruled and gave them birth.

There upon the cultured hill-sides,
     And 'mid vales of fruit and vine.
Dwelt the ancients of my people,
     And in peaceful glory shine.
Children of twelve mighty brothers.
     Who were chieftains in their time,
Dwelt in tents and herded cattle,
     In that land of milder clime.

To that land the spirit led them,
     And upon a mountain hight,
Mid thunder and dread lightning.
     Gave them laws to guide aright.
And His form was like the lightning.
     Thunder bolts were in his hand;
A cloud by day, a light by night,
     He led them to that land.

* This legend is intended to indicate the Indians as the descendants of the
ten lost tribes of Israel.

There they dwelt and grew in numbers,
   In the distant days of yore :
More than stars in heaven unnumbered,
   Or the sands upon the shore,
Grew in riches and in splendor —
   Grew in knowledge, arts and peace ;
Ruled by Kings and chiefs of grandeur,
   While their glory did increase.

After years of peace and plenty,
   After famine, wars and fame ;
Came from out the morning sunrise,
   A King of mighty name.
Shalmanezer, King of Ninus,
   King of city great and proud ;
With his host of mighty warriors,
   To the blast of bugles loud.

Then with fire and sword he ravished,
   All that quiet, peaceful land ;
And his conquering warriors slaughtered,
   With a fierce and bloody hand.
Till the wailing of the women,
   And the orphan'd children's cry,
Rose above the tallest mountain,
   Sobbed and echoed to the sky.

Then the King said, "gather, gather,
   All the ten tribes, great and small,

From the valleys and the mountains,
  And banish one and all.
Lead the captives to the Northland,
  To the ice-clad land of snow :
They the children of the Spirit,
  My wrathful curse shall know."

For the mighty King and warrior,
  Evil King and warrior proud :
Had sent forth this proclamation,
  To the distant nations loud.
" These are my human sacrifice,
  Sent unto the rising sun ;
To the seas far north and eastward,
  They their journey have begun.

" There upon the distant ocean,
  Bright upon the sunrise seas :
They shall glide into the sunrise,
  Wafted by the golden breeze."
Onward marched the gloomy captives,
  Guarded through the distant land ;
Over plains of emerald verdure,
  Over streams of golden sand.

By the wrecks of ruined temples,
  Through the land of unknown gods ;
Through the wilds of many woodlands,
  Where the hunter never trod.

By many an orient city,
  Through many barbarous tribes :
Over snows and frozen rivers,
  Trod the remnant of ten tribes.

Trod and journeyed, weak and weary,
  'Till their tired limbs had bled ;
You could trace their toilsome pathway,
  By their blood and scattered dead.
'Till upon the shore of Waters.
  Did the feeble captives weep ;
As in boats, but rude constructed.
  They were launched upon the deep.

Launched upon the World of Waters.
  As the sun rose o'er its waves :
An oblation to the sunrise,
  Launched both children, wives and braves.
And their captor guards returning.
  Sent across the sea a shout ;
'Till the captives hair stood upward.
  And the rising sun went out.

Then 'mid murky seas and darkness.
  Scattered, desolate and lost :
On the world of mighty waters.
  They were whelmed and tempest-tossed ;
'Till the sun came out in brightness.
  And they drifted to this shore :

But their hair stood up like bristles.
  As it never stood before.

And their faces pale and palid,
  Were dark and red like gore ;
And they journey on and travel.
  And will travel ever more.
The Good Spirit sent them hither,
  Sent them to this silent shore
Where were many bear and bison
  In the hunting days of yore.

Here they roved from North to Southland
  Till they spread o'er all the land,
And they worship the Great Spirit
  Who their fathers did command,
Whose voice is in the thunder
  And who rules the stormy sky.
Whose hand lifts up the mountains
  And sets the stars on high.

We, the red-faced child of forests,
  Are descendants of the gods,
The Good Spirit breathed upon us
  And formed us from the clods,
And when life's journey's ended
  We shall meet the Spirit there,
In the hunting grounds of promise
  Far amid the realms of air

CANTO ELEVENTH.

THE RESCUE AND THE RED PALADINS.

The mountains dressed in robes of snow,
'Rose from the tranquil vale below,
And bathed their brow of snowy white,
Far up in the empyrean hight,
In clear blue sky that bent above.
As if to press a kiss of love.
In whose translucent depths of air.
As rose the sun in splendor fair.
Shone sparkling gems of crystal clear,
Like diamonds 'mid the atmosphere.

The frosty corruscations bright.
Like glittering jewels charmed the sight,
And winter spread her snowy vail
O'er mountain top and verdant dale.
The mountain columns seemed to pry
Into the clouds and prop the sky :
And make a lofty temple grand
Of azure sky and fleecy land.

Oft ere the sun with brilliant smile
Rose up beyond their hughest pile,
Trod Truman **Gray** with footsteps light,
A snowy path 'long mountain hight,
And hastened on with thoughtful mien.
Whose earnest eye, and vision keen
Took in the grandeur of the scene.
He paused now on the mountain side,
And viewed the landscape far and wide,
And scanned with anxious eye the tide
Where rolls Pacific's waves of pride.
Brushed from a rock its snowy crown,
And on its mossy edge sat down.

He oft had journeyed to this spot
To muse, and there bewail his lot.
"Since strength came back, and in yon cave
My home's been with the aged brave,
Oft here I've come," he said "to **view**
The bay and ocean's waves of blue.
In hope some ship might hug this shore,
I reach it—and my wanderings o'er.
But Fate's adverse, these mountain wilds,
And drifts of snow in dark defiles;
And winter's stormy blasts deny
To reach the settlements, I try.
Far on yon waves of shimmering light,
Some distant sails have blessed my sight,

Like gleams of hope they came and passed
To leave a sadder breast at last.
For Hope doth span this sea of life
With all its waves of stormy strife,
As yon cerulean vault of blue
Doth span the rolling waves I view.
And yon majestic surging sea,
Fit emblem of eternity,
Is like man's soul, 'tis never free,
Amid life's storms that darkly lower,
Amid her calmest, peaceful hour,
From strife and rolling tides of thought,
Where rain-bow hues of hope are caught.

" Hope is the polar star of night
That God hath set to fix the sight
And bid the soul look unto Him
Before Whose light the sun is dim—
Whose gaze the solid earth can melt,
As if a thousand suns did belt
Its form with all-consuming fire,
O lift my soul unto Thee nigher,
O kindle Hope's eternal fire,
Thou light across life's narrow sea,
That lights my soul's eternity!"

His was the mind that loved to view
God in nature.   And there he drew

Fresh inspiration, for nature's grace
Seemed more familiar than man's face.
Her beauty pleased his mind and eye,
Infused fresh hope and calmed each sigh,
And bid his heart and faith look higher,
Unto the soul's immortal Sire.

He was not of the sneering kind
Who thought it showed a lack of mind
To acknowledge God as one divine,
Or own the Hand that framed the skies
Was grandly strong and wondrous wise.

Oh Shame! to lift the puny arm,
A throbbing brow, and lip of scorn—
A beat of heart or pulse of brain,
A little span of joy and pain.
A gasp—a breath—we call the life,
And challenge to forensic strife,
Omniscient wisdom who made all.
And central suns for his foot-ball.

Next to revealed and nature's God,
Whose face shone o'er the path he trod,
Was her whose charm of soul and face
Lit brighter lamps of heavenly grace
Within his heart, and there begun
To be affections' central sun.

Like bursts of joy in life's June,
She'd set his song of life to tune:
Whose music through its crystal sphere
Rose like an anthem rich and clear,
To charm with gladness and to cheer.
Next to his God she nobly stood,
Divinely fair, divinely good.

For hours he mused his wandering o'er,
Then saw a ship approach the shore.
He hurried down the mountain side,
And pressed toward Pacific's tide.
The coast seemed near unto the sight
When viewed from off the mountain hight—
Unto the eye seemed scarce as far,
As Ajax tossed a mace of war:
And yet 'twas many miles away,
Scarce could be reached within one day.

He hastened on with urgent speed,
For much he felt an urgent need;
'Till past the mountains, 'mid the hills,
A sudden fear his bosom thrills;
As through a rocky vale he sped,
An arrow passed above his head.
As if by magic in his path,
Three warriors rose with frown of wrath;

Spoke not, but silent red and grim,
With folded arms they looked at him.
A chill passed through his startled blood,
He paused and for a moment stood;
Then leaped the rocks with nimble feet,
And bounded like a reindeer fleet.

Though strong of limb, and swift of race,
The Indians followed not in chase;
But silent for a moment's spell,
One raised his hand and gave a yell:
When o'er the vale and rocky dell,
A hundred braves like magic rose,
And stood like statues in repose.

As if the wizard blast of Duh,
Had raised from earth his clansmen true;
As if the Dragon's teeth were sown,
They 'rose from shrub and tree and stone,
Armed with hatchet, bow and gun;
Surrounded thus, he ceased to run,
Judged from their ambush and array,
They meant to capture, not to slay.

He calmed himself and sought the chief,
And asked if on acquaintance brief
He'd lend a guide to ocean's shore,
That he might roam these wilds no more.

The chief spoke not, but spurned his hand,
And ordered, with a stern command,
The prisoner bound both foot and hand.
Thus Destiny did darkly loom,
A spectre still enwrapt in gloom.
Nor *one* was there, with gentle will,
To smile away each gloomy chill:
While night came down and winds were high,
And fateful clouds bespread the sky.

Next morn the sun, with brilliant glance,
Arose and shook his dazzling lance,
And golden banners did unfurl,
And shivered light upon the world.
The red men 'rose and did advance
To wildly dance the fierce war-dance.

'Ere eve they bring the prisoner 'round,
And to a tree he's tightly bound.
They then stand off and hatchets throw,
As if to brain him at a blow;
And pleased such torture can give pain,
They try it o'er and o'er again.
And then, their horrid torture done,
Demand that he the " gauntlet " run ;
Now, women fierce and warriors brave,
Provide themselves with club and stave,

And form two lines, with space between,
And sternly stand with savage mien.

"Few carry hope who enter there,
Who passeth through their life we spare."
With sinking heart and stubborn breath,
He bounded through this lane of death.
As quickly, sternly, on he goes,
He staggers 'neath the fearful blows,
Showered thick and stern as winter snows.
He presses on through that red host,
He staggers—reels—and all is lost.

But no! marines, from ship on coast,
Rush on them, with a sudden shout,
That put the cruel braves to rout.
This was the U. S. naval ship
"Defiance," on a western trip,
Bound from 'Francisco, up the coast
To visit some new naval post;
From thence, to cross Pacific's strand,
And visit ports in far Japan

A vacant post, with ample pay,
Was offered Truman on that day,
Which he accepted, for 'twas vain
To sooner homeward turn again.
So, o'er the wide and rolling sea,
The ship sailed on majestically.

CANTO TWELFTH.

The day was drizzling, damp and chill,
As the gloomy hearse came up the hill;
Came up the hill in the little vale,
Came where the strickened ones bewail.
With silent tongue to tell its tale
Of man's mortality.   Who can read?
A thousand tongues speak in the deed,
A thousand hearts have need to bleed,
Where wave its plumes, and pause its steed.

What forms once proud, now cold and bowed,
What sunlight quenched by murky cloud,
What nerveless limbs in pallid shroud;
What pulseless heart no longer swells,
But cold within its prison cells,
Its solem pause, its presence tells?
Yon youth with haughty brow and form,
And manhood strong to breast life's storm,
And wrinkled age and beauty gay,
May need it ere another day,
To add clay to its mother clay.

Who hath not in the **solemn night,**
Dreamt that his spirit **took its flight,**
And felt the dismal **hearse** that bore
Him to the grave's unhinging door.
Then felt his heart sink low to hear
The clods that rattled o'er his bier,
And prisoned in his narrow bed,
Torn hair from his despairing head?

Who hath not **in** sleep's fancy flight,
Beheld a gulf yawn in **his** sight,
Of deep unmeasured gloom and **dark—**
A void where **hope could glean no spark—**
And felt his spirit sinking down,
And falling, thought its depths profound;
Who hath not caught a glimpse of death,—
And paused in dream to catch his breath.

On the day before a shadow fell
On the happy home at Eden Dell.
A shadow that falls on every home,
A shadow that dwells in every dome,
In every bright and sunny vale,
In every breath of Summer gale,
In every smile of lovely face,
Bewitching form or charming grace.
Lurks in each bright and laughing eye,
Pursues each footstep passing by.

As the hearse came up the sloping lane,
The sad, pale face of Ethel Vane
Looked out on the chill and dismal air,
While her soul was bowed in hopeless prayer.
And as she sorrowed and repined,
She, weeping, said: "Thou wert good and kind,
Oh, my father, dear! None now can cheer,
For thy form lies cold and coffined here,
Soon to be borne to thy narrow rest
'Neath the clod of the vale. And thy breast
Once so warm, and thy arm once so strong
To protect in thy love, ere long
Shall be dust unto dust, dust, dust.
Life has passed, soul has passed from its clay,
Passed from earth and from sunlight away.
I am fatherless,—orphaned to-day.
Life is brief, hopes are brief—most brief,—
Tears of grief cannot bring us relief.
They but hide the chill earth, like the leaf.

Let us hope, let us love, let us trust,—
For we live, it is life. and we must.
Let us dream there's a home for the just,
Where the soul cannot moulder to dust ;
Where the flowers that bloom never fade,
Nor bright forms sleep for aye in the shade.
And the eyes that are loving ne'er close
For death, or the tomb's dark repose.

Farewell, oh, my father! no more
Shall we meet, lest it be on that shore
Where farewells are spoken no more;
Where the heart that is weary shall rest
In the home, in the Isles of the Blest.
When the dream of this life shall be passed,
Shall we meet, oh, my father! at last?"

And friends stood near, with silent tear
And kindest sympathy, to cheer,
And guarded, as a sacred trust,
The last remains of pulseless dust.
Attending, on its burial day,
The remnant of once living clay.
But living hearts are more distressed
Than those that sleep in throbless breast,—
And eyes that shed the mournful tear,
Than those well closed within the bier.

Ah! what can heal the wounded heart,
Extract from grief its stinging smart,
And bid the sad and troubled soul
Be calm amid the storms that roll?
Not earthly sympathy can fill
The "aching void," and sorrow still,—
'Tis heaven's work the soul to save,
And calm life's tempest and its wave.

And noiseless steps and silence there,
Showed death was in that mansion fair.
And hearse, with sable plume, at door
Would bear what would return no more.
The master of its stately hall,
To two by six of earth,—his all.
Now o'er that face with soft brown hair,
Over that heart so bowed by care,
Was shade of grief and sad despair,
'Twas sorrow's vail of sombre touch.
That showed the heart had suffered much.
Not that dark pall that mourners wear,
To hide the grief they do not share ;
But on the eyes fair azure scroll
Was written sorrow to the soul.
Beaumont, her lover, then stood near.
With others 'round her father's bier,
And strove with sympathy to cheer.

After the service sad and brief,
And hearts were touched with silent grief,
The solemn procession moved away
To where they lay the coffined clay.
Amid the drizzle, chill and gloom.
They lowered it in the open tomb.
" Ashes to ashes," the preacher said
And bowed in prayer above the dead.

11

And here through ages have laid them down,
The wearer of rags or kingly crown.
In the earth they rest, the mouldering dead,
While the world moves on with restless tread,
As it soon will move above your head.
Dost doubt it?   'Tis a common fate,
The seed is planted,—only wait.

*   *   *   *   *   *   *   *

But months fly by, and tears must dry,
And hearts forget each sad good-by.
And cheeks will bloom that grief did waste,
Forgetting sorrow's bitter taste.
The sun as brightly glow and shine,
And other loves the heart entwine,
And other thoughts the mind employ,
While toying with some earthly toy.

And life move on its tread-mill way
As it hath moved for many a day:
Else life would be a darker doom,
Than Tophet's shades or Pluto's gloom.
So live and love that sober grief
Alone, may sadden life too brief;
Nor tear and wound the aching heart,
Let Gilead's balm relieve the smart:
And He who said, "Come, and I'll bear
The burden of thy every care."

*   *   *   *   *   *   *   *

On a beautiful summer day,
A ship rode out of New York Bay,
Rode on, and on, toward the sea,
Like a stately sea-bird proud and free,
While on her crowded deck there stood,
A group of tourists in gay mood.
Then Ethel spoke and raised her hand,
" Look out upon yon beauteous span
Of water's blue and azure sky,
And stately ships that pass us by,
And tell what poetry is there?"
Beaumont replied, " If truth be fair,
Upon the tide or in the air,
The surge of waves, the roll of sea,
Is drear commotion unto me."

Then Ethel spoke with earnest soul,
" The waves in their playfulness roll,
The air has the flush of rich gold,
And the sky seems the earth to enfold,
With curtains of soft azure hue,
Draped and arched o'er a world of sea-blue.
The sun with the fervor of prayer
Looks down in rich splendor so fair,
And the gleam and the glow of his rays,
Like the flush of a cheek at its praise,
Like the flash of a bright rolling eye,
Thrills and warms the soft soul of the sky.

The ships come and go in their glee,
Like worlds on the breast of the sea—
Like souls with a haven in view,
Seem strong to go on and be true.
And the shores basking dim in the day,
Like dark times of old, fade away—
Like hopes that have flown with the past,
Like shadow's dark memories cast."

Then Beaumont said, "I little share
Your love for nature's beauties rare,
And poetry and art, 'tis plain,
Are merely softness of the brain,
A milk and water diet rare,
Of sun-beams, rain-bows, and pure air.

"But you have made," fair Ethel said,
"A sad mistake of heart and head.
The poet's eye was made to view
The beauties of the good and true,
The grandeur of the earth and sky,
And gems of truth that never die.

"Its province is to glad unfold,
The wealth of heart, the beam of soul.
This wealth is greater far than king's,
Or gold, or power's pleasure brings

"Tis bliss of thought, 'tis food for brain,
Who taste will wish to taste again.
And nature's beauties ever stand
The wonders of a matchless hand.
Where lofty minds may walk abroad
And catch bright glimpses of its lord.
As in a temple grand view
Its varied beauties ever new,
And gazing thus the mind unfurls
To beauty richer than all worlds.
And treads the temple of its God,
Like rainbow resting on the sod,
Yet lifting its empyrean head
Beyond where burning suns are fed."

Then he replied: " But is it due
To call exaggerations true ?
His silver linings, golden hues,
His rainbow tints, and crystal dews,
That gloss his fabrications bold :
Is truth diluted—overtold,
The tinsel glitters, not the gold."

" Yes, partly : we'll admit it true.
But poets take a grander view :
Remove the rubbish and the screens,
And look on noblest sights and scenes.
And viewing life 'tis his to see
Oft not what is, but what should be.

For instance, let one take a stroll
Through quiet vales where streamlets roll,
And view a peaceful hamlet there
'Mid sloping meads of verdure fair,
With warbling songsters in the trees,
And balmy fragrance on the breeze.
With modest church spire in the air
Serenely pointing souls to prayer,
And quiet scenes, unvexed by creeds,
Becalm the breast to gentlest deeds;
He says, ' how peaceful, and how fair
This lovely vale and languid air!
It seems a heaven here begun,
Nor sweeter spot beneath the sun.'"

And such it should be, but ah! then
Should he learn this: rude, quarrelsome men
Dwell in that vale, and women fair
Tattle and scatter scandal there;
The flock that seeks the church he viewed
Are torn by faction—cursed by feud

This breaks the charm.   When this we see
'Tis that which is, but should not be,
The poet's mission was to view
What there seemed beautiful and true;
It was the fault of man that there
Was strife where should be peace and prayer.

"True poetry is meant to raise
Truth's standard—point to duty's ways,
To lift the world's eye, bid it view
Earth's noblest joys forever new,
And make such standards and such goals
As fit the grandeur of our souls:
To elevate the plain of life,
Strew flowers amid its sordid strife;
Bid spring's perennial burst and flow
Along the dusty paths we go;
To glad our hearts and cheer our ways,
And point our souls to brighter days.

" There's poetry in earth and sky,
To thrill the soul and charm the eye:
In every star, in every flower,
In every calm and verdant bower;
In every rill that seeks the sea,
In every tone of melody.
'Tis in the bright and sweetest mood
Of all things beautiful and good."
" For your sake I'll believe it true,
But transient as the morning dew."

" Not so," she said, " for this I hold
Thought is eternal as the soul,
And poetry's the life of thought,
And its creations nobly wrought,

Are more enduring than the land—
The hills that rise, the groves that stand.
Earthquakes may level, time decay,
But thought and mind ne'er pass away:
They journey on through endless worlds,
Where souls expand and mind unfurls."

He answered thus: " But then I hold
'Tis useless stuff. What's beams of gold
And silver lakes and Jasper seas,
But ideal nothings—phantasies ?"
" Poetry is useful. It dresses truth
In fadeless beauty, endless youth :
Consigns foul wrong to dark despair,
And lifts the soul that bows in prayer.
'Tis dowered with strength to help the weak
To champion right and raise the meek.
Without its heavenly smile to cheer,
Earth would seem dark and life seem drear.

"And this we know, and this we feel,
'Tis the ideal makes the real.
God thought of earth and it was made.
Man thought of temples ere were laid
Their deep foundations, and in air
Rose up their forms of beauty rare,
Ere shone the sculptors work refined,
A daintier form was in his mind.

And beauties that on canvas gleam
Are but the painter's inner dream :
And ere the poet touched the lyre,
His soul thrilled with his words of fire.
Men oft let grossness pull them down :
Weigh soul and matter by the pound,
Nor seem to know that power of mind
Hath ever ruled and swayed mankind :
And solid matter round it stands
As lumps of clay in potters' hands."

" But see yon ship.   There is a face
Seems bright with some familiar grace.
Upon the deck amid the crowd.
His face all sadly pale, and proud
He stands in manly posture grave.
And gazes here across the wave.
How earnest is his wistful gaze !
I've known that face in other days.
And yet my memory cannot trace
The time. the person, or the place.
Upon the ship I read her name.
" Defiance."   Who knows whence she came ? "

They pause and look, and then renew
Their theme. till ends the interview.
And turning from the deck. they soon
Were chatting in the gay saloon.

For days and weeks the ship rode grand
Far o'er the waves to a foreign land,
Borne by her engine and the breeze
Across the rolling "hollow seas,"
With precious freight she nobly braves
The wind, the tempest and the waves;
Like sea gulls in her flight she came.
"Like a thing of life" she rode the Main.

To ease the sorrows gone before,
Fair Ethel visits many a shore,
Attended by some worthy friends
Whose presence social pleasure lends:
"Does" Europe and the British Isles,
Views London shops and Paris styles;
Looks on the Alps with glaziers grand
And on the vales of Switzerland:
And 'mid Italia's sunny clime
Looks on the pride of ancient time,
Her verdant plains and orange bowers,
Rome's crumbling piles and ruined towers;
St. Peters' spire that towering sits
Above its dome and minarets:
Venice, Vienna, Berlin, Bath,
Lie in the circle of her path;
She strolled where red-ripe suns incline,
O'er vine clad bowers along the Rhine,
And breathed the cool refreshing breeze
From Baltic and the Northern seas.

And while in Rome. on a lovely night.
They went to view, by bright moonlight,
The Coliseum, grand and tall.
And wander through its spacious hall.
Grand, gloomy. there it silent stood.
And they felt the chill of its lonely mood.
Its grandeur seemed the heart to still
And all the soul with grandeur fill,
Which then 'rose up, supremely free.
To grasp for God and sympathy.

The scene was weird and wondrous grand—
The relic of a wondrous land.
Where Rome, proud mistress of the earth.
Held cruel carnival and mirth.
Delighting in the horrid feasts
Of Christians torn by savage beasts;
Defenseless maids, the lion's prey.—
And gladiators wound and slay.
It 'rose so grand. so towering high,
It seemed to arch the very sky.
And lift its walls of mossy stone.
Like ruins of a world unknown.

These two strolled from the rest aside
And sat beneath an archway wide.
Beaumont and Ethel. side by side.
Each, for a time. was strangely still.
While thought and fancy roamed at will.

She mused upon sad memories past,
While *he* admiring glances cast
On her, whose face, in tranquil light,
Shone with angelic halo bright:
And seemed, in sunlight or in shade,
The fairest good the gods e'er made.

And bending near, he did declare
His love and hopes; asked her to share
His love and life—to be his wife,
His guardian angel 'mid earth's strife.
He said: " Amid the wreck and gloom,
Where these vast ruins grandly loom,
He felt companionship a need,
A pulse to beat—a heart to bleed
In sympathy.   That desolation lone
Might never claim him as its own :
Nor ruin brood where joy should smile,
As o'er this solitary pile.

And he, to woman's love unknown,
Though sceptered on earth's grandest throne,
Like this vast pile, doth dreary stand—
A ruin 'mid the fairest land;
For God made woman's noble love
Of pure and rarest joys above,
And put man's earthly heaven in it,
If he's but worthy and can win it."

Then Ethel mused, and answered low:
"The moonlight o'er these ruins glow
And gives dark shadows to the walls;
So memory's twilight sadly falls
Upon the ruined wrecks that rise
Within my heart. Its broken ties,
Once grandly fair, stand sad and drear,
Like shadows o'er these ruins here;
And memories light alone is cast
O'er crumbling idols 'mid the past.
These, all my love and reverence claim,
A memory—what you please—a name:
A dream of bliss, a joy once mine,
An idol wrecked within its shrine.

"I fear not desolation drear,
I'd rather sit 'mid ruins here
And muse on joys that come no more,
Than tread on pleasure's verdant shore.
These scenes accord with scenes within,
The wreck of joys that might have been.
I have no love, no heart to give;
The heart that once did glow and live
Is in a lone grave far away—
Dug 'mid the past. There let it stay."

The moon now darkened by a cloud
Threw o'er the scene a sombre shroud,

And, like the clods thrown on a bier,
Some distant foot-falls echoed clear;
And pausing in the words they said
They heard the watchman's lonely tread.
More distant and more solemn fall,
And echo from the dismal wall.
Then, in the pause, the owlet's cry
Awoke the startled air near by
As both arose.   Each breathed a sigh;
And 'mid the moon-light and the shade,
They vanished as two shadows fade;
Amid the grandeur and the gloom,
Where Rome's proud ruins grandly loom.

CANTO THIRTEENTH.

WHAT SHADOWS WE PURSUE—WRECKED.

Some months before the scene just past,
The ship, "Defiance," anchor cast,
And on that bright midsummer day
Rode proudly into New York Bay.
And Truman Gray, all smiling fair,
Breathed with fresh joy his native air.
And stepping on his native shore
He thought to turn and roam no more:
For life preserved he breathed a prayer
For help that came mid dark despair.

He'd been in ports of far Japan.
Of China and of India's strand;
'Mid Orient climes and yellow seas,
'Mid ardent suns and balmy breeze;
'Mid gorgeous splendors. heathen fanes,
Where cruel lust most cruel reigns;
Where all is fair in land and clime
But man becursed with every crime;

And trodden 'neath Ambition's sport,
Crushed down by priest and Juggernaut,
At Superstition's base command,
Bound mind and soul, bound foot and hand.

Had crossed the surge of waters where
Cape Horn roars from her stormy lair
And lifts her pyramid of rock
To breast two ocean's solid shock,
To part their surging tides in twain,
And crowned with storms not breast in vain,
But stand the monarch of the main—
A granite wall that God did grow,
Saying " Thus far—no farther shalt thou go,
But here this granite pile shall stand
To part the waves on either hand,
A tower of adamantine worth,
Built on the solid ribs of earth."

He'd seen the thick Brazilian wood
Where rolls the Amazonian flood—
This inland sea, this mammoth strand
Of ocean flowing through the land,
The mother of a thousand streams,
The sire of almighty rivers :
Where hastening seas of waters gleam,
And dancing wave in sunlight quivers.

Whose Sylvas grandly tall and green,
Of every gorgeous shade and sheen,
With birds of rarest plume between,
Crown her the forest's empress queen.
This garner of the streams that run,
This ocean in a continent,
This changing mirror of the sun,
Where crescent moons smile sweet content.

Where forest kingdoms richly loom
Entwined with vines of brilliant bloom,
Where graceful palms enchain the sight,
And grasses forty feet in height—
Scenes that no pen hath yet unfurled
In tints of beauty and of splendor.
'Tis gorgeous as a rainbow world
Begirt with hues of rainbow splendor.

Young Truman gladly pressed again
The land that he had left with pain,
And soon from friends he heard and knew
What he had dreaded, feared was true.
That Ethel Vane from New York Bay
Had sailed for Europe on that day,
And that the one that fixed his view
Was her fair form and eyes of blue,
That on the ship that passed him by,
Had held entranced his anxious eye

And caused her then to strive to trace
Remembrance of his wistful face.

Early next morn he took a ship,
One swiftest on an ocean trip,
And hoped to reach New Foundland strand
Ere the other ship had left that land.
If foiled in this, to seek her smile
And join her tour of British isle.
His ship plowed swiftly through the main,
And yet to him it seemed in vain
Her iron lungs sent forth the steam.
She seemed a monster in a dream
That slept amid the water's gleam.
He wished her speed had wings that flew
More fleetly than the winds that blew:
And skimming fast the briny sea,
Kept pace with his expectancy.

Two days—three days, and still she trod
The ocean like a winged god,
And oft upon her deck he stood
And wistful scanned the rolling flood.
The next day rose bright, fair and clear,
But ere the night sank dark and drear,
So that he sought his room for cheer
There cast him down upon his bed
To rest his thoughtful, throbbing head,

And Morpheus' arms did gently creep
Around him, till, in slumbers deep.
Sleep threw the mantle of its charm
O'er love's unrest and fear's alarm.

How long, he knew not, ere the day
He felt the shock, the ship did sway
And tremble.   Then, as if to gain
Her feet, she plunged amid the main.
And now they look o'er ocean drear,
And every face is pale with fear :
And women shriek—but most are still
Like bosoms stunned too deep to thrill ;
And strong men shake with pale affright—
Some call on God, some moan with might,
While others neither fear nor feel.
But seem transformed to pulseless steel.
The quaking timbers groan in grief.
And tremble like a storm-tossed leaf :
And in her breast of steel and wood,
She seemed to feel the angry flood
Tear at her heart—a lunge, a splash—
Her timbers fall with fearful crash.

Then Truman Gray. with pallid brow,
Saw surging waves rush o'er the prow.
Sweep wildly, madly o'er the deck
And toss and whelm a sinking wreck.

Then seized a broken hatchway door
And as the angry sea rushed o'er,
He launched it on a stormy wave,
The only hope his life to save.

And 'mid the roaring rushing sea
And 'mid wild shrieks of agony,
Of hopeless prayer and helpless moan,
Of struggling death, and gurgling groan,
That stately ship once strong and brave
Sank 'neath the stormy whelming wave.
The port she sought she ne'er did gain—
She rides no more the stormy main.

She braved its storms for many a day,
And came and went from bay to bay ;
She caught the winds that freely roam,
She made the blue waves dance with foam
As white as snow flakes in the air,
And carried old and young and fair,
And many a hope and earnest prayer ;
When Oh, alas !   One tempest night
When all was dark to earthly sight,
While steering on her pathless way,
She struck where foaming breakers lay
'Twas night—she never saw the day,
And ne'er again trod ocean's way.

The wild waves shrieked above her grave
And many were the fair, the brave,
That from her living breast she gave.
Some rose from pleasant dreams to sip
Unwelcome waters at their lip,
Some, scarcely rousing from their berth,
Thought nightmare held them to the earth,
While waters cold as winter's storm
Rolled darkly o'er their breathless form,
And wondered fancy thus could seem,
And dying thought it all a dream.

*   *   *   *   *   *   *   *   *

Far out upon old ocean's flood,
In hopeless, sad despairing mood,
With parched lip, and shivering form,
Truman still hoped through wave and storm—
Hoped that these dangers he might brave
And heaven would rescue and would save;
And thus he said :   "Two days have fled
Since I have tasted drink or bread,
I'm almost famished ; and since night
No passing ship has blessed my sight.

"O, God! my refuge and my rock,
'Mid storms that beat, and waves that shock,
Save, save me from these depths profound
Where I am sinking down, down, down ;

Unmeasured depths beneath me yawn,
Infinite heights above me fawn
As if to mock my hopeles fate,
And blast, a speck from time and date."

"Borne by the current and the breeze
He floated toward the northern seas;
Two stormy nights, three stormy days,
Was tossed upon dark watery ways.
Weary, doubting, and in distress,
Nor food to cheer, nor hope to bless,
The third day's light did slowly fade,
The third night lower its dismal shade,
And as it settled o'er the deep,
He fell in an exhausted sleep.
The waves then quieted, and now
The stars looked down from heaven's brow,
And saw him rocked upon the deep,
Cheerless and cold in feverish sleep;
Clutching wildly his frail sea barque—
A waif that floated amid the dark.

And thus he floated on and on,
'Till the gray light showed the rising dawn,
Then, quick aroused by sudden shock
That made his frail boat quake and rock—
He woke.   The stars of silver hue
Shown in the sky and waves of blue;

The surf lay in their beds asleep,
And silence brooded o'er the deep:
He looked, and saw a crystal isle
Rise just before with cheerless smile;
Like mount of glass with sloping side
That sailed amid the drowsy tide.

It was an iceberg island grand,
That floated from some northern strand—
Now 'neath the gleaming stars alone,
A sea becrowned with jeweled throne.
He was beside it so he 'rose
In deep despair from sad repose.
And, clambering up its rugged side,
Viewed sky and ocean far and wide—
A king upon a crystal throne,
A monarch of dread wastes unknown.

And still he gazed and still rode on
Amid the gay and purple dawn,
There slaked his thirst with calm delight
From snows upon that crystal height—
Snows soft and pure as childhood's kiss,
And fair as maiden's smile of bliss—
The crystal snow with peerless glow
That fell from heaven to plains below.
Unknowing if 'twould turn to mire,
Or cool the lips else would expire.

And now he saw the clouds unfold
And dress in purple, red and gold
To meet their ardent lovers gaze—
The morning sun, with genial blaze;
Whose coming made the waters smile,
As rosy as a playful child,
And sparkle in their depths of blue
With braided tints of rainbow hue;
And glitter like a thousand stars
Were woven with its rainbow bars,
And yet, coquettish as a maid,
Would blush in gold of every shade
And smile in every rose's hue
That God hath kissed with sun and dew.

And there upon that crystal height,
He viewed the liquid circle bright
And wondrous, fairy, crystal isle,
Where peaks rose in fantastic style
And vales and clifts in grandeur stand,
As ne'er was seen on isle of land.

Three miles in length, it calmly lay
And floated on its watery way,
A mile in width the sight did greet,
Tall cliffs that rose a hundred feet,
And slow the isle did melt away,
Meandering south from day to day.

And Truman felt strong hunger's pain
While wandering o'er this icy plain,
And, as he passed a rugged knoll,
Above his head he heard a growl,
He turned, and saw a polar bear
Spring at him from his icy lair.

He drew his jack-knife, stepped aside,
And as it lit he probed its side
And planted oft the steel again,
Till warm blood bathed the icy plain.
They struggling, fell—'twas hard to tell
Whose bones would strew the icy dell.
The bear seemed clumsy, and his weight
To doom him to the darker fate.
At length the steel was plunged so stout
It reached his heart and the blood flowed out.

And the dead bear lay neath the golden day,
And Truman knelt as one to pray,
But hunger's strong, and starving pain—
He, kneeling, drank the blood of the slain
And felt its warm life thrill each vein.
Starving he ate, nor thought it wrong.
On food, as prayer, the soul grows strong.
He ate its flesh and took its hide,
And round his outer garments tied,
A mantle warm, the fur inside,

Partook his breakfast—juicy, **rare,**
Of liquid red and soft, warm bear,
Which much improved his strength and mood,
And seemed, to him, delicious food.

Oh! ye who taste the dainty wine!
And on rich viands **feast and dine;**
Ye scarce can know what nature craves
When palates **yearn and hunger raves!**
Ye know not what **will bless and cheer**
The hungry when no better's near.
And dainty **sons of wealth and ease,**
Like him would **hunger thus appease.**

And there three days he lived and sailed,
And oft his dreary fate bewailed—
Lived on the bear that he had slain
And melted snow from icy plain.
The fourth day now began to smile
Above this glittering, icy isle,
As he strode up its slippery hight

To see if any sail in sight.
And there, his sad **soul to** beguile,
He mused on destiny awhile.
There, seated on his icy throne,
And viewing that dread waste, and lone,
He said   ''The hopes on which we stand
Are like ice-ships and ropes of sand—

The sun will shine, the winds will blow.
And then they vanish like the snow.

" And life is like that Person who
Our Saviour to the mountain drew,
And promised all the world so fair
If He would bow and worship there.
We bow and worship.   Then we view
Our rich possessions.   But mildew
Is on their fairness, at their core
The blighting worm, the cancer sore.

Each pleasure has its sting of pain,
Each joy we garner seems in vain.
The cypress with the laurel wave,
And death's the glory of the brave.
Joy, fame, and wealth soon pass away,
Those meteors of a stormy day,
Those idols of a longing heart
We dream are balm to ease its smart."

" Fate's iron hand seems on our life
And we are pigmies in the strife;
Our hearts are torn and taught to feel
They should be stone incased in steel;
That we should check life's ardent glow.
Throttle ambition. pride, and show,
Eject love's cancer from the breast.
With its dark brood of doubt, unrest

And worn with grief, our brows bend low
Down to the dust, till thence we go."

But hark!   He hears a grating crash,
A lunge a tremor and a splash.
The icy hills are torn and hurled
As if an earthquake rent his world,
And that fair isle that lately smiled
Is made a plunging monster wild,
And rent into an hundred isles
Of icy heaps and glittering piles.

The peak on which he stood before
Shook to its base and turned half o'er,
And cast him on an icy heap,
That surged like billows of the deep.
The cold waves and the ice did chill
His body with a sudden thrill,
And 'mid the heaving fragments tossed
He deemed all hope was lost, was lost.

Now struggling from that seething pile,
He gained a small and rugged isle,
And clambering up its slippery side
He deemed this his last earthly ride;
His bruis'd limbs were too cold to smart,
And a dark chill crept near his heart.
He thought " Soon, dreary and alone,
A corpse shall float this waste unknown,

And I shall solve this problem deep
If spirits rest, if souls can sleep;
That problem that hath puzzled man
Since time was young, since earth began;
O'er which the wise and brave hang fears
And earth hath wept a sea of tears.

"Soon I'll unlock 'mid these dread seas
The mystery of mysteries,
And drop down that abyss of gloom,
That's dreadful in its voiceless doom,
Step forth into a void unknown,
Sail o'er a dark sea, silent, lone,
And when gone hence, return no more,
Breathe not earth's air, cull not its lore :
And in all ages yet before
Tread not again time's sunlit shore.

"This mystery I must shortly try,
The sting of death *is mystery*—
A darkness spreading o'er the brain,
A dullness where there once was pains,
A stillness in the throbbing breast,
A beamless eye, a heart at rest,
A light gone hence—forever gone,
A night where reigned a cheering sun,
A spirit fled ; where ? We know not—
A gasp of breath and earths forgot.

What next?   **Who** knows?   Perhaps a dream,
A lightning flash, a silver gleam;
A sunshine far beyond the night.
A spirit treading worlds of light;
A silence broken 'mong the stars.
The universe in spangled bars
Of rainbow beauty, and **bright hues**,
With music dropping **like the dews;**
An anthem through the joyous years
Saying ' Here's **the end of death and tears,**
And here's where joy and hope unfurls
As dreamt by souls in other worlds.'

"Or woeful fate, from death's dark doom
Sink down to depths of endless **gloom,**
And deeper night, where wild despair
Can breath no words of hope **or** prayer ;
And where the God of Gods unknown,
Except to curse his spotless **throne ;**
Where comes no ray of hope **or** light,
But one eternal starless night.
God save a soul from such a fate
Nor let repentance come too late.**"**

But **heavens!**   His stiffened limbs and sore,
Can hold his freezing weight no more,
While slipping slow above the sea.
He hangs in hopeless misery.

Breathes his last prayer and lifts his eye
To look his last on earth and sky :
Then sees a ship slow sailing by.
" Help ! mercy !" was his feeble cry
And then he fell.   A hungry wave
Received him to its liquid grave ;
And kissed him with its lips of foam
As greets a wife her husband home.

CANTO FOURTEENTH.

A RETURN—A FAREWELL.

On a bright, rosy evening in June,
A songster was warbling a tune,
In the evergreen branches above,
A troubadour's song to his love :
While the fountains leaping with spray,
And the flowers that smiled to the day,
Seemed to tiptoe to catch but a note
That fell from the sweet warbler's throat.

'Twas where one would linger, to tell
Of the beauties of fair Eden Dell
Whose mansion in loveliness rose,
And basked in the sunlight's repose.
In its parlor all costly and fine,
With windows rich trellised with vine.
Where roses and lilacs in bloom
Wafted into it sweetest perfume ;
Beaumont bowed him low to his love
And gazed in her fair face above.

His form it was manly and tall,
But his eye seemed to lure, then appall,
And lack that sweet frankness and grace
That shines from the soul through the face.

"O bid my sorrows all depart,
Grant me," he said "but half thy heart,
A gem that's worth this earthly ball,
How could I hope to win it all.
O! smile on me with generous grace,
Thy image I can ne'er efface,
'Tis written on my inmost heart.
Have mercy, do not bid me part.
Pity the heart that's sad distressed,
Pity the soul in its dark unrest,
Pity the sore and wounded breast
Smote by the dart thy hand hath pressed.

"O! bless the soul where thy image bright
Hath rose like the sun o'er its world of night.
My love hath shrined thy image fair,
Its hope its heaven and its prayer.
Wilt thou accept its proffered aid.
No consecrated fane or shade
E'er held an idol such as thee,
Or such a worshipper as me.
My heart's a gorgeous waiting fane
And thou its idol. O, remain!

My soul like ancient earth's in night
O, speak its chaos into light."
He paused.   She reached her hand, a tear
Shone in her soft eye bright and clear,
Her breast shook with a trembling sigh
Of tenderness and sympathy.
She raised him to a seat the while
And smiled through tears to see him smile.

" The flag is lowered, the battle done,
What love hath won is nobly won."
And then the tear that would not stay
Was gently, sweetly kissed away ;
And yet that cheek still felt the stain
Was something sadder than a pain,
Because it had been pressed before
By him, alas ! who came no more.

O, gentle heart of woman true
That drops in mercy like the dew,
That falls in blessings like the rain,
To cheer and soothe another's pain,
Who ever sought from womankind
Some love or sympathy refined—
Sought once, twice, thrice, but what she rose
To lift to gladness and repose.

Though some have scorned a second plea
And in their wrath would turn and flee,

And call her fickle, heartless, proud,
And mouth her defects far and loud.
No ear more ope to mercy's cry,
No breast so touched by sorrow's sigh,
No softer hand, more melting eye
Than woman's, true and tenderly.

Within the tree top sings the bird,
Beside the gate a step is heard,
And Truman brushed the lilac bloom
And snuffed with joy the glad perfume.
He thought of parting by that gate,
Nor doubted time, nor questioned fate.
His step was quick, his soul was proud,
His glance fell on a fleecy cloud.
He said :   " 'Tis like the cloud that passed
Before the moon when we met last.
I thought it was an angel fair.
One soared above, one stood just there :
I know an angel dwelleth here,
I know this is an angel's sphere ;
Within this cultured Eden fair
I feel her breath upon the air."

He paused by window wreathed with vine,
He saw another's arm entwine
Round plighted idol of his heart ;
His soul leaped up with sudden start,

And then he hears with deeper grief
These fearful words so plain and brief:
" My plighted one, I view with pride
The day thou'lt be my loving bride.
How soon the day when we shall wed ?
A month—a week ? " " Ah ! more," she said,
"Two weeks to-day, my love, we'll wed."
" Two weeks ?" said she, " but then 'tis fit
That I learn early to submit."

"O, deathless love, and hope of years,"
Young Truman said, " farewell with tears.
To enter there would be unkind,
To longer stay would make me blind.
Who could endure what e'er betide
To see another claim his bride—
To see another's arm entwine
Her waist, like tendrils 'round a vine.
I came to seek love's soothing rest,
To fold a loved one to my breast.

" Like dove that wandering, turns too late
To seek an absent cherished mate,
And finds a cruel hawk's been there
His mate to capture and ensnare :
So fate has chased me o'er the earth
Nor left me mate or cheerful hearth.

Oh, that my life by sailors brave,
Had ne'er been snatched from ocean's wave."
He turned, it was no Eden now
For care was written on his brow.
He turned more cursed as unbeloved
Than Adam when with one beloved
He turned from Eden.   Such is love.
With heart benumbed and foot-steps fast,
He down the rosy twilight passed.
His mind was feverish with unrest,
Oft to his brow his hand he pressed :
Old scenes familiar to his eye
Seemed as in dream to pass him by,
And through old streets, and haunts well known
He passed, and thought them strangely grown.

But useful pride brought some relief
To chill his love and soothe his grief :
And ere he ceased to walk about,
He deemed his love was quite crushed out.
Alas! love is a mightier power
Than can be crushed within one hour,
Or in a life of years; for oft
This gentle passion true and soft
Glides through the years three score and ten,
And warms the breast of hardest men.
When Truman turned his room to share,
He met his friend, proud Maud St. Clare.

"Ah, Truman glad to see you back,
And trust your welcome naught will lack.
In your far travels westward, say
Have you e'er met young Hugh McVeigh,"
She blushed.   "You've seen him then—'tis years
Since I had heard; I had my fears
That he was dead.   He was a friend
I meant not to displease—offend,
And yet he left in angry pride."
Then Truman pausing, thus replied:
"Far out upon the plains one day
While shielded from the sun's bright ray
Beneath a tent, he did unfold
The secret of a love untold.
You were the object.   To his mind
You were too haughty and unkind.
Repulsed his love, nor bid him think
That to your image he could link
One tender thought of hope or love,
This brought despair, and made him rove."

"O! he was wrong, what him despair?
No man was blessed with love more rare.
I did repulse, but 'twas to see
And test his love and constancy."
"'Twas sad, 'twas very sad to see
The bitterness and agony
As he and Earl Darring, side by side,
Told of their love and sullen pride.

Earl Darring when a fair haired youth,
With eyes of blue and heart of truth
Returned from college, but to find
His plighted one had been unkind.
To see her to another wed;
From haunting memories then he fled."

" Ah! Pauline Golden," she replied,
" A year ago her husband died.
She loved Earl Darring, yet was taught
To mind her parents, and she thought,
That she must marry whom they said
Regardless how her bosom bled :
And then she heard with jealous ear,
That he another held more dear.
But 'twas untrue, for oft it's so,
That rumor's false as fiends below.

" Deception is a blighting curse.
Detraction is a curse that's worse.
Of all the curse on human kind
A slandering tongue's the worst we find.
Deception was my fault of old—
When most I loved my look was cold.
For fear my thoughts would speak aloud,
My mien was haughty, cold and proud.
'Tis writ in Truth sent from above :
· Without dissimulation, love.'

Had I but heeded, many a pain
Had passed to ne'er return again."

Then Truman and fair Maud depart,
Each musing with a saddened heart.
He to his chamber quickly went,
There, by his window seated, leant
His chin upon his hands, to gaze
Upon the sunset's fiery blaze.

And musing sadly, thus he said,
With bitter heart and bended head :
" I love to think how very sweet
It is to feel the warm heart beat,
To feel the red lip pressed to lip,
And like the bee the honey sip,
To feel two hearts together beat,
As one times music with the feet,
To taste the cup more rich than wine
From juicy clusters of the vine.

" And yet I say, and count the cost,
'Twere better to have loved and lost,
Than, like the beast that treads the stall,
To never love or sigh at all.
'Twere better to have seen the sun,
And felt new life and joy begun
Though blinded by its dazzling light,
Than always to have dwelt in night.

" 'Twere better to have lived, though strife
May mar the hasting hours of life—
To feel the warm and breathing soul,
Though sorrow bid its tears to roll.
Than dormant in the womb of night
A nothing known to life or light
That God hath spoken unto birth,
To view the sun or tread the earth.

" For on creation's ample breast
There is a spot where souls shall rest,
Far, far beyond the strife of time
A heaven eternal and sublime.
· I've wandered like a waif astray
And suffered, useless, day by day,
And like that 'much-enduring man.'
I've been storm-tossed by sea and land,
But when returned, 'tis not for me
To find a fair Penelope."

Then, as the blood-red sun went down,
With aching heart he sat him down,
And, on the bitter moment's spur.
He wrote and sent these words to her :

FAREWELL.

We parted forever.   No farewells were spoken—
I breathed not a sigh and I gave not a token
That the heart thou hadst wounded, the hopes thou didst sever
Had bid thee farewell through time and forever.

Though it shrouded my heart in darkness and gloom,
As I folded my love as one laid in the tomb;
I felt that no anguish, no sorrow or pain,
Could make it return to its idol again.

I have buried it deep, where the willows ne'er weep,
No shaft marks the tomb where its ashes doth sleep,
And Memory herself shall forget the dark spot
Where I laid my first love to be spurned and forgot.

For I seek that rich jewel, a heart that's above
The worship of Mammon, and knows how to love.
But thou never could'st prize such a jewel of worth
As the heart's true affection—rarest gem of the earth.

When I came in proud joy with love's ardent haste,
Another's fond arm twined around thy fair waist.
From her strong plighted faith he had won my fair bride
And they cooed like the doves as they sat side by side.

As I turned in my sorrow, with care on my brow—
I ne'er had cursed woman, and will not curse now—
But I felt that the Eden, from man taken away,
Was snatched from my grasp by a woman that day

May oblivion's dark waters wash out every spot
Where thy image was known — even thy name be forgot.
May thy lover be cold as dark shades that entice.
Or the iceberg that dwells in thy bosom of ice.

In thy future of life, when thou hopest to be blest,
And thy heart turns to love, as a dove to her nest,
Mayest thou feel the keen pang of a heart that is spurned,
Or a love that is fickle and coldly returned.

Hath wealth wooed thee to win thee with glitter of gold,
For they say that heart treasures are bought and are sold,
Accept such a proffer, no envy is mine
For a heart that sells love or bows at wealth's shrine.

We have met—I have loved—We have parted forever.
I've suffered—I'm strong, and glad now to sever.
I seek not thy love, and will not—no, never.
We've parted in time—we've parted forever.

CANTO FIFTEENTH.

MISFORTUNES—A DIGRESSION.

As day declined and shadows fell
O'er embowered Eden, in Eden Dell,
A lover passed to the mansion gate:
'Twas Beaumont Jerome now blessed by fate
His look was pleased, his eye was bright,
He smiled there in the soft twilight;
His lip still felt the parting kiss,
And in his soul there dwelt the bliss
Of love requited.   Such is love.
'Tis sunlight from the heavens above.
There is no sweeter joy or bliss,
There is no brighter heaven than this,
Amid this world of grief and pain
Than to love, and be beloved again.
He felt it though his sordid soul
No higher measure knew than gold.
He deemed the day's work nobly done
And view'd the match a golden one.

He scarce beyond the gate had passed
When on a youth his eye he cast,

Who passing said, "Doth here dwell
Fair Ethel Vane of Eden Dell?"
" Yes, and the note hand thou to me."
" I will not, what is that to thee?"
He snatched the note from out his hand
And sent him off with stern command.
" I will deliver this " he said,
Then turning opened it and read.
The boy walked off with sullen look
While youthful wrath his bosom shook.
Beaumont Jerome, ah! well you passed
And plucked the note from out his grasp,
If handed to the one he loved,
'Twould Truman's long thought death disproved.
Then as the light of evening fades,
He passed adown the evening shades.

Upon the morrow came a friend
To borrow news or gladly lend,
As women sometimes love to do
If rumor tell her story true;
And to fair Ethel said, " Your friend
Soon brought his visit to an end."
" What friend? Young Truman Gray? Ah. me!
I thought him dead. It cannot be
That he has lived and ne'er sought me."

So when her friend had gone away,
She sought her room and wept that day,

And said, " In other days he trod
'Mid verdant bowers o'er emerald sod.
And fed on nectar like a god.
And must I doubt?   He said he'd rove
To show and test his changeless love;
He'd love me—love me well and long
With love eternal as the song
Of shimmering stars, or blazing sun
Whose smile of love is never done.
Ah me!   Such is the lover's part;
The tongue speaks stronger than the heart.
And false vows have no bitter sting;
Lip-service is an easy thing."

To-morrow came, its new-born light
Spreading above the shades of night,
Lit Ethel's room with kindly cheer,
And kissed the darkness from that sphere.
She rose, with weary heart oppressed,
For feverish dreams disturbed her rest,
To find in horror and amaze,
Her beauteous Eden home ablaze.
To see the burning cinders fly ;
To see a red glare belt the sky ;
To see the fire-fiend lap his tongue,
Leap out and rave, and hungry run
Along the house and to her room,
And puff his smoke and toss his gloom.

Ha! how he laughs and waves his brand
With red perdition in his hand.
Ah! now he grasps the roof on high,
And now the cinders whirl and fly ;
He breaks the roof in, now, oh, fly!
There is no time to think or sigh.

Then, from the blazing building red.
For life she quickly turned and fled.
Then standing, saw in sad afright.
Her home consumed to ashes white ;
Naught saved from fire's consuming waste,
But some apparel snatched in haste.

But such is fire : when on the hearth
It glows and smiles in childish mirth ;
'Tis like a friend that's good and mild ;
But let it madden and grow wild,
But let a spark the chimney throw
Upon the roof. where breezes blow,
'Twill seize a house and crush it in
And frolic like the god of sin :
Nor will it aught of value prize,
There's nothing sacred in its eyes.

A few days after this sad fate,
As at a neighbor's she did wait,
This direful news came.   Her estate
Was bankrupt, and her guardian late

After bad management and waste
Had took her all and fled in haste.

An orphan—both her parents dead,
A child to ease and fortune bred,
Her beauteous, fragile mother died
Ere she had been three years a bride.
Her father was a man of wealth,
A merchant, who, for ease and health,
Improved his home so rare and well,
He named and called it Eden Dell.

'Twas in a city's suburbs, where,
Crowning a vale of beauty rare,
It stood upon a central knoll
That sloped to where bright streamlets roll,
There, in its noble grandeur, stood
The stately mansion fair and good.

And porticoes, enwreathed with vine,
Did cluster round the mansion fine,
And emerald meads on every hand
Stretched to where groves of beauty stand;
Hollies, magnolias, forest trees,
Waved here their branches to the breeze;
And shrub, and rose, and lilac bloom
Breathed forth a rich and sweet perfume,
And honeysuckle arbors blend
With bowers that cooling fragrance lend.

While oft above a pebbly pool
Hung graceful willows bending cool;
And fountains shoot their silver spray,
And shower their gems through all the day.

Ethel, an only child, and so
When he had died, two years before,
Inherited his large estate,
And, young and fair, seemed blessed by fate.
And Truman was the lover true
She favored, and her father too.
Their fathers had together roved
In youth, and the same woman loved.

But she denied his father then—
She could not marry both the men.
An angry quarrel then ensued
Which doubtful friends urged and renewed.
Until their heated blood ran high,
For honor's wounds some one must die—
For but a word, an angry breath,
They each must face a willing death.

A challenge sent—an answer came:
Pistols—ten paces—seconds' name:
Place—the church-yard on the hill.
Six loads—and shoot until we kill;
The time—sunrise to-morrow morn:
I face the sun and you the church forlorn.

The morrow's sun rose fair and grand—
Ten paces off they take their stand :
Two pistols in the sullen grasp
Of hands oft pressed in friendship's clasp.
The second speaks : "One—two—three—fire"—
But hark ! A voice rings clear and higher :
"Stop ! God forbid," and rushed between.

They turned, with quick and startled mein,
And saw their loved one standing there
With tearful eyes and flowing hair,
Between them, so that neither can
Shoot at or hit his shielded man.
She wildly urged, she shamed she plead :
"When you look on the other, dead—
Slain by your hand—how could you dare
To look on me or the sun up there ?
'Tis barbarous —sinful. Stop ! Beware !"

They feel her words, they each relent,
Before her pleading beauty bent
Their stern hearts and their stubborn will,
Till kinder thoughts their bosoms fill.
They drop their pistols, droop the head,
Till kindly she together led
The life-long friends. An hour before
Each was to each a mortal foe,

But now she gently lays one's hand
Within the other's, and they stand
Two friends, led by an angel hand
From wilfull murder, human gore,
To friendship more faithful than of yore.

A friend had told her of the plot,
When, in wild haste, she sought the spot
And by her valiant deed did wed
Two noble hearts that else had bled.
And coming years taught each to see
Her life was love, peace, purity.

Now, when a dreary week had flown
O'er Ethel Vane, so sad and lone ;
And sordid Beaumont, having found
Her fortune gone, with grief profound,
Sent her this cold and cheerless note,
Which seemed in hottest haste he wrote :

" Pardon my long delay to call
And that no word I've sent at all.
By sudden business called away,
I have been absent till to-day.
Enclosed find letter that was found,
I hasten now to send it 'round.
I learn your lover is not dead
And now, of course, we cannot wed."

" How mean and cruel," then she said
And ope'd young Truman's note and read;
And then she wept; for more than all
This wrapt her heart in darkest pall.
Like Man of Uz, in times unknown,
Misfortunes did not come alone;
And when her heart was most bowed down,
Faith viewed afar a starry crown,
And, by religion's golden ray
She gazed on realms of fadeless day.

Religion, pilot of the soul
To heaven's fair fields, where bright unfold
The Jasper sea, and streets of gold,
The tree of life, and streams of joy
That death and pain can ne'er alloy:
Communion with the spirit's sire,
A coal from out the altar's fire;
A gem from off the tallest spire
Of God's all wise, eternal love
That lifts the soul to His above,
Consumes the dross, refines the clay,
'Till winged with bliss 'twould soar away.

She felt religion's soothing touch,
Though much she suffered, it soothed much;
Its deep and rich consoling power
Threw hallow 'round that suffering hour—

Threw light above the lowering night
And fixed a star to guide the sight.
Through suffering's fire the strickened soul
Rose up to seek a higher goal,
And in its seven-fold heat was tried,
To come out tempered—purified :
Then, having put her trust in One
Who is the soul's bright central sun,
Sweet peace came down upon her head,
She rose in tears while thus she said :

" All joys of earth must pass away,
All fortunes crumble and decay,
All hearts must feel some bitter pain,
All bliss must turn to grief again,
And very sad indeed to some
Does love with pensive sorrow come.
When hearts must still their bursting grief,
O'er faded joys so bright and brief.
And those that should sit side by side
Are wandering far o'er land and tide ;
When soul from soul. and heart from heart
Have long been severed—torn apart,
And life, that should be joy, delight.
Is turned to darkness and to night.

" But, such is life, pursued by Fate ;
Grief comes to all—some soon. some late.

In youth, we step with buoyant air
And dream all earth is bright and fair—
The flowers bloom, birds sweetly sing
And life seems one bright joyous spring ;
But, when a few bright years have flown
And we are older, wiser grown,
The rosy hours of youth, no more
Come back from o'er time's dusky shore ;
And then, we see life's barren field
Can naught but transient joys yield.
For we are transient pilgrims here,
Oppressed by doubt and chilled by fear,
Who cross the hills where flowers grow
To rest within the valley low.

" For hopes will fade, and hearts will burn,
And souls for highest bliss will yearn,
And love will have its wanderings here ;
Earth brings us all some bitter tear,
And they who seek for perfect bliss
Must seek another world than this."

CANTO SIXTEENTH.

THREE FRIENDS HAVE MET AGAIN.

The sun his course had almost run,
And twilight shadows, dark and dun,
Began to sink o'er prairies wide,
As sinks the strand 'neath ocean's tide,
When far from down a mountain road,
A horseman on his charger rode,
And urged with roweled heel along,
His plunging courser, swift and strong.
His form swayed with a haughty mood,
His actions showed he was pursued ;
And yet his fearless mien and eye,
Belied that he was forced to fly.

He sat erect, defiant. grand,
Looked back and shook his clenched hand,
And speeding fast as winds can blow,
Still hurled defiance at the foe.
His steed leaps o'er the rugged earth
While foam flies from his dripping girth :
With hoof of steel and heart of ire,
Strikes from the rocks their sullen fire,

And spurning earth beneath his feet,
Skims o'er the mountains swift and fleet.
And swift, and swifter grew his speed,
For ne'er had steed more noble need
And still with panting nostrils wide,
Feels rowels plunging in his side.
While his pursuers, pressing fast,
Are distanced by each moment passed.
Until they halt with sullen mein,
And turn unto the mountains green.

Young Truman still his flight pursues,
Until he in the distance views
A train encamped ; then, pats with grace
His charger. as he slacks his pace.
At length beside a tented train
He halts, and drops his courser's rein.

At once, from out a tent that day,
Earl Darring came, and Hugh McVeigh.
And soon beside his steed they stand
And grasp him with a friendly hand.
They three, upon the plains before
Had met, and talked their history o'er

"How now, old friend, whence comest thou ?"
"Too tired to tell you all just now,
But in the mountains, over there,
I thought to hunt some deer or bear,

But, straying from my comrades far,
I stumbled into Indian war."
"Come, enter here and sup and rest.
We still are roving in the West,
And glad to meet upon the plain
Our well remembered friend again."

They enter then within the tent
And there the night and evening spent,
There ate their supper, rude and plain,
With appetite that none can gain
But those who've breathed inspiring air
Upon the prairies vast and fair.

There, 'neath the tent upon the plain,
Talked o'er the days of yore again.
They two then unto Truman said:
"Three swiftly-gliding years have fled
Since last we met.   Thou art not wed?
Thy lady fair has proved untrue,
Just as we said, for well we knew.
So lift the hand unto the sky.
Swear life's a cheat and love's a lie."

"I will not, though I sought my bride
And found another by her side.
But this I learned and tell to you,
Where one is false there's two that's true.

And you of all men last should be
To doubt a woman's constancy.
I found your love—the proud brunette,
With queenly form and eye of **jet**—
Pure as the gold that's fresh from **mint**,
True as the steel that cuts the flint.
And this she said—said Maud St. Clare :
' **No man** was blessed with love more rare.' "

" Good heavens!" then Hugh McVeigh replied,
And shook the tent from side to side.
" Woe, woe is me for now I see
That we have suffered needlessly.
My ardent love made me dispense
With all I had of common sense,
For 'tis the first thing lovers spare
And I am no exception rare.
But with to-morrow's rising sun,
To her my journey'll be begun."

Then Truman to Earl Darring turned
And said, " I accidentally learned
That she **for whom thy bosom burned**
In early youth, is now unwed
By death.   Her nearest friend this said :
'At parent's stern command she wed,
While Pauline Golden's bosom bled
With early love, true love for you.'
So, for one false there's two that's true.

Earl Darring slowly then replied,
With sober thought, and gently sighed :
" Long years have flown since on the day
I pressed her hand and strode away.

" Since then the years have brought to me
The all I love—a memory—
A phantasy that haunts the brain
Like gleams of starlight on the main :
And there, at recollection's door,
They enter, sadly bending o'er,
Like mourners at a tomb, they seem
To weep above a vanished dream.

" Methought I saw a heaven afar,
An Eden with the gate ajar
Through which I thought to pass, when lo !
An angel frowned.   Can it be so,
That angels frown with haughty pride,
And thus an entrance is denied ?
I trembling turn, for lo ! I see
I am debarred by fates decree.

" And yet, perchance I might have won
A heaven, had I but ventured on.
I, turning, thought as I gazed there,
'Twas beautiful, 'twas strangely fair.
It came—it went, and memory cast
Its beauty on the faded past.

I thought not memory'd give me pain
By turning oft to look again,
And love would burn in fancy's blaze,
And gazing, turn again to gaze.

"Such dreams, alas! they come to all,
And chase sweet visions we recall,
Like butterflies through memory's hall.
And memory's magic touch can bring
To faded flowers the hues of spring,
To withered hopes the bloom of youth,
The charm of beauty and of truth.
For memory's sweet enchantments rise—
A rainbow, spanning earth and skies,
A world of beauty that survives—
A heaven within our inner lives.

"But ah! if memory's visions bring
A dream that hath a waking sting,
That Eden hath a serpent there
To tempt to madness or to prayer.
And fruits forbidden ever rise,
More fair, more charming to the eyes.
Such, such is life, mind will unfurl
Some spirit dream from spirit world.
Some image, seeming more than thought,
Some lightning gleam that fancy caught,
Unknowing why, or whence it came,
A dream too wonderous for a name.

'Tis yearnings of immortal souls
For higher bliss, and brighter goals,
For fairer heaven, and sweeter joys
And peace serene that naught alloys.

"If I have drempt a dream like this,
That mocked me with untasted bliss,
Few knew it, and full thousands more
Have drempt that very dream before.
Life yields us little, though we drain
A brimming cup, 'tis mixed with pain.
Fate's hand hath stirred its bitter draught,
Else higher heaven we ne'er had sought.

"But saddest thing beneath, above,
Is burial of the heart's first love ;
To fold it as the silent dead
Within the shrine where it hath bled—
Its throne and tomb.   Beside it there,
Grief's monument, and pale despair ;
Fond memory bending near to brood,
With drooping wings and tearful mood
O'er desolation drear and sad,
O'er hopeless hope so wild and mad ;
A sigh congealed amid the gloom,
A cypress drooping o'er a tomb,
As cheerless as a sphynx's smile
Forever gazing on the Nile.

Yet every heart, like every town,
A graveyard hath—where it lays down
Its withered hopes and vanished joys,
Its faded dreams, and follies toys,
To hide them from the light **of day,**
Where they may moulder **to** decay.

"**So,** since the years have brought **to me**
A dream **of hope,** from memory—
Another's palm hath fondly pressed
The lilly hand I oft caressed;
Another's form hath clasped the breast—
"Twere heaven had it been mine that pressed—
Another's lips hath drank the wine.
And left me but the cheerless vine—
Hath sucked the fruit and left the rind.
At feasts, the first's the better wine.
She was not true as thou hast said
To love the one, the other wed;
What! worship Satan for love of God?
Such truth's untruth, though Jove should nod.
I'm older now, perhaps more wise.
No man should sigh deep plethoric sighs,
But champion his heart's enterprise
Like a brave knight—be prudent wise.
Bow not like slave or devotee
To senseless gods; but make his plea,
Then stand like isles **amid** the sea

And front the storms.   The heroes part
'Mid shattered wrecks of proudest heart."

And thus they talked till rosy light
Grew gray and faded into night,
While darkness her dun mantle spread.
Of dusky gloom and shadows wed.
While sleep her opiate dews distilled
And every breast with silence filled.
And love came then with rosy dream
To kiss the joys that seem, that seem.

*   *   *   *   *   *   *   *

As rose the morning sun next day,
Far eastward rode young Hugh McVeigh,
While passed the slowly moving train
Far westward o'er the level plain.

CANTO SEVENTEEN.

UTOPIAN DREAMS AND LOTUS LEAVES.

From out the chambers of the morn,
Aurora, goddess of the dawn,
With jeweled fingers did arise
To climb the ladder of the skies,
While, purpling on the orient blue,
The sable night her form withdrew.
And opal shadows gaily dance
Along the hills as they advance.
Like fairy sprites of light new born
That weave a chaplet for the morn
Then, glowing on the azure plain,
Like heralds of a monarch's train,
Upon their steeds of dapple gray
Advance the heralds of the day.

'Twas when the weeks and months had rolled
Their checkered wheels of gloom and gold,
That as the sunlight kissed the dawn,
Young Truman rose and faced the morn.
And saw the glowing hues of day,
Spread o'er the prairies far away,

Like rosy dawn of early love,
When cupids 'mid the flowers rove.

He said. "Last night, in slumbrous dream,
Soft, loving eyes did lustrous beam
Into my own.   And on my cheek
I felt warm, joyous tears that speak
The melting heart ; lips touched to mine
As soft as rose leaves—bliss divine !
Pillowed upon her soft warm breast
My head I gently, sweetly pressed
And felt the pulse of love beat free
As yearning wild waves of the sea.
Heavens ! I was prouder than a king,
Empires ne'er such raptures bring.
Each kiss was worth a thousand pounds,
Each tear a planet load of crowns.

"This was my kingdom. ne'er to part,
For I was lord of the loving heart.
Was Antony wise?   For such bliss
He gave an empired world like this.
Had Alexander's hopes thus furled
He ne'er had wept for other world.
Had Mary's love a Byron blest,
His life had been a sea at rest—
Not casting up foul earth and mire—
A ship that sailed a sea of fire.

A genius burning with that love
That makes a vulture or a dove.

" Fi! who can not be rich in dream—
This mirage of the things that seem,
Sleep's strange sight-seeing telescope
Of things we wish and things we hope.
The untrained soarings of the mind,
That still will wander, unconfined,
And bid the soul still for a time,
View new creations, scenes and clime.
And memory's touch and fancy's hand
Can paint a world of rainbow land.

" In fancy, I have trod the sun,
And empires, queens and battles won,
And painted heaven so grandly fair,
It seemed perfection's answered prayer,
And boundless bliss could scarce unfold
The myriad beauties fancy told.
Yet 'bove them all, in my fond youth,
I prized the loving grace and truth
Of one proud heart.   O days of youth!

" While others thought on fame and wars
And burned to mix in strife and jars,
I loved to 'front the solemn stars
And, with a calm and thoughtful brow,
To measure what life's hopes allow,

And, with my glowing thoughts, to build
Such temple as the soul might fill.
And if on earth or heaven above,
I found that temple built of love.

"On earth God built two hearts as one—
Love's temple, smiling to the sun—
Ordained the family circle ties
The nation's strength—God's wisdom wise,
And men of high or humblest part
May win this kingdom of the heart.
And there times sweetest pleasures bring,
And every man may reign—a king:
Yet not to wield a tyrants sway,
But rule by smiles as rules the day.

"And I have thought—what man has not?
That he was blessed with happiest lot,
Who, turning from a world of care,
Found a true home and wife to share
The comforts that his toil might bring,
Where joy could smile and love could sing;
Where, with sweet, charming grace, a wife
Might soothe the stormy scenes of life,
Becalm the brow, like quiet seas
That hush the billows and the breeze.
Be love upon his life impearled,
Be angel of his better world.

Methought, in dream, that such an one
Smiled on me like the rising sun.

" For such. I'd dare the cruel curse
Of thirty tyrants, doubly worse
Than reigned in Greece.   I'd break the front
Of iron war, and bear the brunt
Of all earth's battles.   I'd burst the bars
Of prisons, lasting as the stars
And built of mountains of blue steel,
And ribbed with adamant, nor feel
The weight of all earth's sceptered power
Though dungeoned in an iron tower.

" And in her noble cause for good,
I'd write my name and fame in blood
Upon earth's iron heart.   O'er turn
Her toppling thrones, and proudly earn
Her worthy praise.   For love can learn.
I'd toil up to fame's topmost rounds —
I'd build a pyramid of crowns
And climb therefrom up to her love
As to a heaven — nor look above
For higher bliss.   For such is love.

" I'd rather win her than yon star
That glitters o'er morn's smiling car.
With isles and continents like this
Forever singing in their rounds of bliss ;

Than diamond mountains rearing higher
And reaching to earth's central fire —
Than treasured heaps of miser seas
And ocean's countless gems—where breeze
Ne'er stirred a ripple; where no wave,
Hath kissed them in their island cave.

" I'd rather dwell in a lone isle,
Lit by no sunshine but her smile,
Kissed by the moaning amorous sea,
From traffic's world, uncursed and free,
Wrapt in old ocean's giant arms,
There feed my soul upon her charms
Than dwell on thrones and fear alarms.
I'd feast upon her beauty fair,
As God's ear on the breath of prayer;
I'd drink the starlight of her eye.
As sun's the haze of summer sky.

" As lakes kissed by the soft moonlight,
I'd bathe my soul in sweet delight,
And earth ne'er drank warm crystal tears,
As I such bliss through coming years
And ne'er grow old : but young, like truth,
i'd taste this fount of fadeless youth.
I'd woo her as the stars the sky—
As woos the moon, with loving eye
The sighing earth ; as spirits free
Woo worlds of light and destiny.

" I say it.   I affirm it o'er
Though it be drowned by traffic's roar,
There is a love unbought, unsold,
Oft times unuttered and untold,
That in this world of sordid sense
Hath not reward, or recompense,
In all the round of fleeting years;
God's eye, alone, may see its tears.

" Last eve, I saw a nameless grave
Upon the trackless plain.   It gave
No sign upon its verdant crest,
It held within its pulseless breast
The ashes of immortal fire—
'Twas silent as the cloud capped spire
Of old Cathedrals.   Then me thought:
All yearning souls shall taste this draught
Of utter silence—nor their name
Nor hopes, nor whisperings of fame,
Nor record of their life or birth
Be known on this forgetting earth.

" And then me wished it was my part
To slumber in its mouldering heart,
And feel my pulse as dumb, and still
As shadows on the distant hill.
My throbbing heart, now pulsing brave,
As quiet as that lonely grave.

That slumbering in the pale moonlight,
Peered up into the vault of night.

" Upon a day I scaled the cliffs,
And on the cheerless snowy drifts
Lay human bones, all bleaching white ;
An eagle just had taken flight,
And screamed above my venturing head
As if to fright me with the dead.

" I said, 'more cursed are these white bones
Than those that sat on marble thrones !
If human flesh makes eagle mirth,
Or feast for worms in groveling earth,
What matter ?   If the soul's at rest
This funeral pyre—this mountain crest
'Is grand enough to hold my breast
Until it bleach like driven snows,
And tombless be its dust repose ;
An eagle feeding on its prey ;
A white speck on a mountain gray—
A spirit soared far, far away.'

"For sorrow's winds have blown me through
As through the night air drops the dew :
In the rent fissures of my heart,
Departed hopes like adders start,
And cypress and the willows wave,
As if that spot contained a grave.

"O, doting heart!   I've scarce begun
This sage soliloquy to the sun,
Till love is served, in whole or part,
And fed on by my hungry heart.
Be cursed! thou spirit from above,
I vowed to never dream of love.
For bitter fate has sternly taught
My heart to curse its baneful draught;
This gushing stream of fancied bliss
Is but the gall of bitterness.

"This God-like passion, heaven-born,
So was Satan.   His brow of scorn.
Drank heaven's ineffable delight,
Her beauties blessed his godly sight.
Yet he was cursed, the king of woes
He makes perdition where he goes.

"And so does love though heaven-born
If scorning, or if turned to scorn.
If all the sky of ether blue,
Had subtle poison well mixed through,
If all the waters of the sea
Were nitrate silver, mercury,
It were a scare more baneful fate,
Than love that's turned to bitter hate.

"It must be wrong.   And I will think
There's sweets still on that flowery brink

Of doubtful joys.   Uncertain bliss
That borders on a dark abyss.
I just have learned *she* is not wed
But single and her fortune's fled.
I'll write and tell her of my love,
That cruel note, and why I rove."

Then seated on a gentle knoll,
He did unfold his writing scroll;
His noble steed that grazed near by,
Now left his grazing and drew nigh,
And on his masters lap did lay
His head, and with his eyes did say,
" This is your desk, now use I pray."
So on his head of dapple gray
He laid his scroll, and wrote away.

His steed and the immortal there,
Seemed each the other's thoughts to share.
The steed looked with a sad appeal,
And seemed to think and seemed to feel.
Poor beast! to die and pass to mould.
Poor man! the vastness of the soul
Makes longing hearts; where sorrows roll.
One to a deathless future goes,
And one to endless dust repose.
One must on ceasless yearnings feed:
One on content,—that one the steed.

Animal content, and soul rest
Men seek ; but few are blest.
'Tis doubtful if the soul can rest :
It's wings immortal oft will try,
To scale the Heavens—'twas meant to fly.

The letter finished, he spoke thus,
" A lover is a curious cuss
Of rare extremes.   In wisdom's ways
He seldom stumbles—seldom strays.
The warm heart makes the heated brain,
A feverish man is scarcely sane.
Where is the man so mad as he,
Who loves a woman fervently ?

" The sunset streaked with beams of light
Our parting hopes, that dawned as bright,
And purpled on the future view
The dreams of youth that grew and grew,
And love arose and hues unfurled,
As fair as ever blessed a world ;
And gorgeous were the skies of blue,
That brought a fairy realm to view.
But winds arose, and clouds spread o'er
And darkness vailed a stormy shore.

" Tossed by the billows of the past,
Mid present trials, hope may last :

The weary heart may cease to roam,
Affection build her glittering dome
To shade her joys from heat of noon,
Protecting flowers that fade too soon.
And when the joyous day shall end,
And evening shadows gaily blend,
It's sunset sink in crimson, gold,
Where opal-tinted hues unfold.
Then let me hope for such a noon,
And night without a waning moon,
And rosy twilight's peaceful ray,
May follow such a stormy day."

CANTO EIGHTEENTH.

TRIED—PURIFIED.—A COINCIDENT.

Mid golden scenes, and rosy hours,
When hearts sit 'neath refreshing bowers,
While kindest friends surround us here,
To soothe, to comfort, and to cheer;
And fortune smiles, and hope sings sweet,
And streams of joy flow at our feet,
And hands are near 'mid pain or grief,
'Mid pleasures or 'mid sickness brief
To smooth our path, to soothe our care,
And bless with love's attentions rare;
'Tis easy to say " ne'er despair,
Nor hope, nor joys, nor friends bewail,
And ne'er give up the ship, or fail."

'Tis easy for the ship to sail
When seas are smooth, and skies are pale,
Nor let the waves its prow o'erwhelm,
Well manned, and pilot at the helm;
When wafted by the gentle breeze
O'er peaceful waves in quiet seas,
But, when the stormy billows roll,

And arms are helpless to control,
And nerves are quaking to the soul,
'Tis harder then, with clenched lip,
To breast the storm and hold the ship.

And so, when sorrow's billows flow,
And fortune frowns, and friends are low,
And hearts are bowed in bitter grief,
And out-stretched hands find no relief,
And desolation's dismal moan
Wails through the heart, so sad and lone,
That sits beside Hope's dusky tomb
And broods as shadows o'er night's gloom :
O ! say if such thy pity share,
" Look up, and lift the soul in prayer,
To weep is Christ-like—not despair."

And so it seemed to Ethel fair,
With sad blue eyes, and soft brown hair.
Bereft of fortune, wealth, and friends,
Those bubbles of a life that ends.
Forsook by lovers once so true,
And summer friends that once she knew.
O, fortune ! Tyrant of the wheel,
With heart of flint and hand of steel,
Who turns and high or humble kneel,
Who rules the world with stern disdain
Regardless of man's weal or pain.

Who turns her wheel, and jeweled crown
Bows low and drops its jewels down,
And scepters fall from nervless hand,
And peace or war, shines o'er the land.
And wealth, which brings its brood of care,
A promised means of pleasure rare.
A valued good when rightly used—
A soul destroyer when abused.
A blessing when the heart's above.
Low, sordid lust, and glows with love,
And shows the kind fraternal mood
Whose bliss is found in doing good.

And many friends in prosperous hours,
May sit with us 'neath cooling bowers ;
But when Fate's sun our bowers fade,
They seek some other cooling shade—
For gold can make them, as it oft hath made.
But what is fortune, wealth, or friends,
To one whose heart, and hopes and ends
Are compassed by almighty love,
That lifts the soul to joys above—
Where, in the golden city's gate.
Comes neither fortune, wealth, or fate
To canker love within the heart,
Or pamper joys that soon depart.
And so fair Ethel felt, the day
Those transient pleasures fled away

She must the needs of life command,
By toil of brain, and work of hand;
So when a school select and good
Was offered her, with cheerful mood
She did accept, and firm resolve
She would the trying problem solve,
Whether 'mid toil and earnest strife,
The strained and feeble threads of life,
So warped and sore within the breast
Could e'er be wove again to bless;
Or, if that harp of thousand strings
Could ever feel the hope that sings,
If once those cords were strained or broke
That had responded to love's stroke?
If they could cause again to roll
The joyous music of the soul.

So, oft she trod from day to day,
With sober feet, the broad highway
That led to duties well performed;
And youthful minds, with lore adorned.
And they who gazed and passed her by
Observed a sadness in her eye—
Saw, resting on their crystal scroll,
A shadow reaching to the soul,
From whence, thrown on its azure screen,
Like haze above a summer scene—
Its mellow tinge and pensive touch
Showed she had loved and suffered much.

Those pensive orbs of heavenly blue,
Like wells of thought, deep, rich and true,
Showed in their depth of crystal springs,
The softness such as sorrow brings ;
And in their sky-blue tides that roll
The lingering sadness of the soul ;
While glowed upon her features rare
A look that was a silent prayer ;
And nestled on her forehead bright
A sadness sweeter than delight.

Thus as she walked, all like a queen,
Her look was modest, mild her mien ;
Her form, like Hebe's was moulded fair,
Her smile was sweetly sad.   Her hair,
Dark brown and soft, it rippled rare,
Like glossy sunbeams nestled there ;
And round her presence seemed to be
An atmosphere of purity.

One morning, as she trod the way,
Her lips spoke what her heart would say ;
" Last night I gazed upon that star,
And, ere I knew, in slumbers far,
I dreamt, that on an island strand
I was pursued by pirate band.
Coarse, horrid oaths they hurled at me,
I feared their curse more than the sea.

And strained my speed to find a grave
Beneath the ocean's moaning wave.
But soon my limbs had spent their force,
While on my neck rough hands, and coarse,
Were rudely laid, and, on the ground
I felt myself forced down—down—down.

" I struggled in my wild despair,
And breathed to heaven a hopeless prayer,
When, lo! a knight in bold array,
On foaming steed, rode to the fray.
In plated mail, with polished shield—
A nobler knight ne'er charged a field.
With lance, undimmed by useless rust,
He pinned each pirate to the dust.

" Alighting, me he gently raised
And with new rapture fondly gazed—
Smoothed down the ringlets of my hair.
His visor raised, and nobly fair
He stood a hero on earth's sod,
And smiled upon me like a god.

" He pressed my hand until I feel
His pulse beat through the links of steel.
He said, ' I've trod the world so wide,
To find my queen, and promised bride.
I've earned a kingdom and a crown;
I am a prince of high renown.

And I will joy with proudest mien,
To see thee crowned, my noble queen."

" I knew his face, those features rare
Were on my heart and in my prayer.
The scene, the bliss my speech destroy,
My silent tongue was dumb with joy.
He ordered then his vassal train.
They brought a steed with flowing mane,
Then in his arms with pressure sweet
He placed me in the saddle seat.

" Then vaulting on his noble steed,
We passed through woods and flowery mead
'Till on the banks of winding stream.
The castle's towers did grandly gleam
Majestic in its towering front,
To brave the storm and battle's brunt —
The moat, draw-bridge and castle dome,
Seemed fit for grandest kingly home.
The draw-bridge crossed, the gate we passed,
When martial music smote the blast,
And clarion notes rang rich and clear
Upon the raptured atmosphere."

" The morrow dawned and bliss records,
Came queenly ladies and brave lords
In grand attire and noble mien,
And I was crowned the lovely queen.

And as my king of high renown.
Placed on my head the jeweled crown.
And smiling to the assembled peers,
Said, ' Now's the summit of my years.
I crown her, 'tis my loving part,
Queen of my realm and of my heart,'
When lo ! the crown rolled off like stone
And shattered on the ivory throne."

" My heart leaped wild to hear it break,
And starting from my dreams, I wake,
To find it all a vanished dream :
While shimmering through the amber gleam
Of watching stars, I view the while
The islands of the blessed smile,
Far off beyond the midnight sheen
Of earthly hopes.   Where faith is seen
Like light house on the shores of time.
That shines afar o'er worlds sublime ;
Like star-light o'er a sea of gloom :
Like sunshine in a darksome tomb.
And love in sleep is not forgot,
Such dreams are maiden's common lot.

" And in my younger, brighter years,
In day-dreams I have dropped warm tears
Of love upon a manly face,
And in a clear blue eye did trace,

My image mirrored on the soul ;
It's queen, it's heaven and it's goal.
'Twas face not like Apollo's wear,
With cataract of golden hair,
And maiden's eyes of saintly blue,
And cheeks as smooth as maiden's too.
Nor yet Adonis like in mould,
A polished marble fair but cold,
Nor coarse as Mars, nor stern as pride,
Nor Hercules in bruin's hide.
But pure of heart, and brave of soul,
Built on a proud heroic mould.
As true as steel, as fair as light
And strong to champion truth and right—
A soul as guiltless as the sun,
Through which with lighted lantern, none
Would ever need to search for truth,
Or earnest will, or honest worth.
A soul as broad as Heaven's span ;
True nature's god like noble man.

" I do not ask a stately form,
That loves to breast the battle's storm,
I do not ask a titled name ;
A proud heart sighing after fame.
I ask a calm and fearless eye ;
A soul that dares to do or die—
I ask a noble earnest face,
With smile of love and manly grace—

I ask my name be on his heart,
My life be of his life a part,
And written on his memory's scroll,
My love the poem of his soul,
A poem time can never mar,
' As round and perfect as a star.'

" My earthly dreams have been like this,
If Heaven deny me such a bliss;
Methinks in fadeless worlds afar,
Our souls shall sparkle as one star,
And on the hills of perfect bliss,
We'll taste the joys unfound in this,
And drink our thirsting spirits full,
And when our soul communion's dull,
We'll wing our angel spirits far,
Through every universe and star :
And while we rest, and while we soar
We'll taste new joys forever more ;
And sail with spirits glad and free,
A thousand worlds of destiny.

" If soul be soul, if spirit power,
Can reach beyond the dying hour :
Our loved shall meet us and be pressed,
Unto our bosom's fond caress,
Else why the prisoned hopes release,
Else can our yearning souls find peace,

Or heaven—or endless perfect bliss?
If in that fadeless world I miss,
His presence, heaven's charming bower,
Will shrivel like a withered flower;
And through a myriad worlds sublime,
Relentless as the flight of time,
I'd wing my deathless spirit free,
And seek him through eternity.

" And if in all the worlds of God,
I find not foot-prints where he trod;
Like Noah's dove my weary feet,
Would seek that ark of last retreat ,
Unknown to souls—that dismal barque,
Non-entity, destruction dark.
Seek sweet Oblivion's seas that roll,
To still the heart and drown the soul."

*   *   *   *   *   *

Within a city's suburbs, where
Proud wealth had built her mansions fair,
'Mid bright spring days, mild, fair and cool;
Fair Ethel taught a prosperous school.
Dwelt with some friends in mansion fine,
Embowered 'mid trees and blooming vine ;
'Twas Hugh McVeigh, so kind to all,
Polite and courteous, manly tall;
Ardent in speech, firm though polite,
With frankest eye, and keenest sight;

And Maud St. Clare, the proud brunette.
His dark-eyed wife with hair of jet.

As all at table sat one day,
Thus to his wife spoke Hugh McVeigh:
"I have a letter just received,
From Truman Gray. My friend is grieved,
And wants to know if I can tell,
Where dwells the maid of Eden Dell."
A blush came o'er the teacher's cheek.
As for a moment none did speak ;
"When we together roved the west,
He twice to me his love confessed
For this fair maid, while we discussed,
Her faithless love, his foolish trust :
And bid him swear life was a cheat,
And woman's love a base deceit.
But he was firm and still would hold,
While there was dross, there still was gold.

In other days but this he'd tell.
'He loved the maid of Eden Dell.'"
Then to the teacher, "Now her name.
He writes in full and 'tis the same,
If I mistake not, as your name."
She said "I once did live and well,
At my old home at Eden Dell ;
When he came back I thought him dead.
Had mourned him two years as the dead :

Else had I ne'er my trust denied,
Or been another's promised bride."

Then Hugh McVeigh wrote on that day,
And mailed the same to Truman Gray;
The letter never reached the hand,
Of him upon Pacific's strand.
Thus Ethel learned he lived was true ;
And when no answer came thereto,
She sought her uncle in the west,
And then in doubtings and unrest,
Resolved to see the land of gold,
And there her lover's fate unfold.

CANTO NINETEENTH.

TWO SCENES AND A CHAPTER.

'Twas sunset.   From the skies afar
  Pour down the golden rills;
The sun, upon his crimson car,
  Slopes o'er the western hills
And lays the grasp of his red hand
  On mountains glowing like a brand,
And spreads the wild glare of his rays
  'Till sky and plain seem all ablaze.

The distant Rocky Mountain hights
  Their lofty ranges show,
Like white fires on their battlements,
  Blaze forth their caps of snow.
Far on the plain's extended sheen,
  Like specks of white, two trains are seen;
On Colorado's plains they stand—
  This prairie schooner caravan.
One pointed East, one pointed West—
  And this the scene, as thus they rest.

Near by the train that's westward bound
　　Are stalwart men and brave,
Who, in a little group, stand 'round
　　A fresh and new-heaped grave.
A sturdy pioneer that morn,
　　Who held all Indian guile in scorn,
Strayed from his train, ahead,
　　When Indians in the tall grass lay,
And, from their ambush, shot him dead—
　　Robbed, scalped and left him on the way.

So now they halt, at set of sun,
　　And dig a lonely grave,
And left a heap of nameless clods
　　Upon the prairie wave.
His son, a noble boy of ten,
　　His wife and niece were near.
O, when was grief so dark as then,
　　Above an earthly bier ?
No words were read, no words were said—
　　All bowed in grief above the dead.

The boy had spent his grief in sobs,
　　And now, through falling tears,
His eyes flashed like two glowing stars
　　Amid the distant spheres.
He sprang and knelt upon the grave—
　　He raised his hands on high,

As if his soul, for vengeance, gave
  A vow unto the sky:
" Cursed be the dastard, savage foe
  That laid my fearless father low !
A thousand curses on their lives,
  Their lands, their children and their wives!
May Heaven, with red-hot vengeance, burn
  And smite these sons of Cain,
And, from yon fiery, setting urn,
  Fever and famine rain !
And here, I, on my father's grave,
  Eternal vengeance swear
When manhood's gained, no lurking foe
  Shall my true rifle spare!"

He lifted his fair, boyish face
  Toward the setting sun,
That threw the splendor of its grace
  O'er this heroic one.
No Hannibal, in fiery youth,
  Swore vengeance on proud Rome,
With more of grandeur or of truth,
  Nor drove his vengeance home,
In after years, with greater zeal—
  None made the murderous savage feel
That vengeance followed at his heel
  So deadly and so stern, as he
That now, in sorrow, bent the knee.

They sought to lead him from the grave :
　　He clung the closer still,
As if his father he would save
　　And strove his place to fill.
His mother plead with sobbing prayer;
　　His cousin Ethel, young and fair,
Threw back the ringlets of his hair
　　And bid him now return.
Within her own she took his hand
And smiled through tears so sweet and bland,
　　It made his bosom yearn.
O ! she was fair.　Perfection's prayer
　　Of beauty ever shone
Upon her peerless features, rare
　　As jewels on a throne.

He rose and said, " O ! Ethel, dear.
And will my father never here
Come in his strength with smile to cheer.
　　Nor fondly bless us more ?
Beyond the scenes of sunset here
　　You say there is a shore
Where souls are free from death and pain ;
But will he never come again—
　　Come never, never more ?
Was God so good, and yet he stood
　　And saw my father slain ?
O ! could I spill their savage blood,
　　I'd deluge all the plain."

" Ah, child! you little dream or know
How man hath caused man's blood to flow.
And vengeance—it is of the Lord's;
Yet man hath made it whet his sword
And drink the marrow of his foes,
And in a thousand fields and feuds
Hath dealt its deadly blows.
Yet God is good.   Beyond the sun
Trust when this course of life is done,
The soul will lose its woes.
And as the cycling ages run,
Find endless, sweet repose."

She led him gently by the hand,
And men and women of the band
　　In silent tears return.
The sun went down an orb of fire,
Yet threw the red glare of his ire
　　From out his vanished urn.

And now the wife in sorrow knelt:
The brave boy in his bosom felt
　　That day that vengeance gave
New fever to his youthful veins,
An anguish, deeper than all pains,
And dried the scalding tears he wept.
He stole away that night and slept
　　Upon his father's grave.

*   *   *   *   *   *   *   *   *

Behold the moon! the fair, full moon!
  Her silvery shield exalt,
And shimmering through the shadows soon
  Walk up the starry vault.
Within the train whose silent face
  Fronts t'ward the rising sun,
Lying beneath a tent you trace
  A sick and feverish one.

A group of men stood at his feet.
His brow was flushed with fever's heat.
And straying from its dwelling far
  Regardless of the will,
His mind seemed as a wandering star
  That silence could not still.
And fancy led his thoughts away
Where reason threw a flickering ray,
And wild distorted visions grew
And vanished as the morning dew.

The moon arose with pale white face,
And threw the soft light of her grace
  So lovingly and free,
Upon his throbbing feverish brow,
And woke him from his dreams, and now
  He wildly said: "See, see!
She is coming, see her coming

Through the rift of twilight bars.
From the vale beyond the sunset,
    In the island of the stars.
From the cloud beyond the mountain,
    I can hear the music swell,
Angel voices singing sweetly
    As the chiming of a bell.

"'Tis the Eden where I loved her—
    'Tis the maid of Eden Dell.
And my soul is torn to fragments
    By the anguish of the spell;
For the words that she is singing
    Is forever fare thee well.
In the heaven where I am dwelling
    Thou canst never hope to dwell."

" O! the purple dawn of morning
    Shall I never see again?
Must the darkness feed upon me
    As I wander in my pain?
Must I drink the lurid lightning
    Like fresh water from a spring,
And its fires burn within me
    Yet my heart be taught to sing?

"See! upon yon firey billow
    Climbing up a blazing crag.

Is a black and scoffing demon
  And a grinning, toothless hag.
They are scoffing at an angel
  Smiling through a cloud above —
'Tis the one that I have trusted ;
  'Tis the angel of my love.

" But the Heavens dissolve around her,
  And a thousand trumpets swell,
For the loveliest of the angels
  Is the maid of Eden Dell."
He ceased.   A footstep near the tent
  Paused softly in the course it went,
And sweet as music on the sea,
  A soft voice spoke, " 'Tis he, 'tis he."

What charm hath made that bosom swell,
  And lit that glowing eye ?
Was it the name of Eden Dell,
  That caused that startled cry ?
She entered, and the stalwart men,
  Stood back as she passed by.
They thought the angel of his dream,
  Had dropped from out the sky.

" O! Truman dear! and are you here ?"
  Then from her eye she brushed a tear,
And knelt beside him there.
  She laid her hand upon his brow,

She gazed into his eyes, and now
She seemed to be in prayer.
" And is my face so strangely grown
Your Ethel is to you unknown ?"
She said in sad and plaintive tone
As rolled his vacant eye ?"

His soul seemed to have caught a strain
Strange and familiar, yet in vain,
Remembrance could not make it plain,
   He knew not whence or why.
He tried to think, he tried to rise,
He scanned her wildly with his eyes,
And said " No more, I see a shore,
Where men are wading in their gore.
   What gashed and bleeding ones !
And feeding is the carion crow,
As they walk ever to and fro
Upon their dripping bones.

" No no, this ugly scene is o'er,
Heaven's streams have washed that dismal shore.
   And they are angels : see them soar !
Lo ! it is resurrection's morn—
See how the bones dissolve in scorn
   To pure ethereal clay,
As through the vista of the morn,
   Bright winged they soar away.

17

" Behold her eyes stream from the skies,
    Like the gleam of a glowing star,
And her angel spirit sweetly rise,
    Through nebulous mists afar.
And through the dawn of new-born day
Bright wings have come to bear me away.

" Away—away!" His head fell back,
His eyes, like meteors on their track,
    Flashed wild and bright.
At length the soft light of her eye
Charmed like a soothing lullaby,
And her kind voice, so sweetly near.
Fell like soft music on his ear,
    Enchanting as delight.
Her gentle touch, her dainty tread,
The moist cloth laid upon his head,
    Love's silent glance, the dropping tear,
Brought stillness and a quiet cheer.
Her dimpled hands now caught the power
    To calm him in delirium's hour.

And there she watched the fever's strife
And nursed the flickering spark of life,
And bathed his brow the long, long night,
Nor thought of rest or sweet repose
Until the morning sun arose.
Then, early in the glowing day,

As moved the westward train away,
  They led her, with resisting plea,
From where her sleeping patient lay,
  Almost as sick and wild as he.

*   *   *   *   *

One week had rolled her days of gold
  Along the path of time,
While, shimmering through the amber fold
  Of skies that bend sublime,
The sun from out his hights of old,
  Rode through his azure clime.
Young Truman on his charger rode
Along a rugged mountain road,
  And oft repressed a sigh.
He rode in haste, though it was clear
'Twas not from danger or from fear—
  No fear could daunt his eye.
The startled bear within the wood,
The prowling wolf that snarling stood,
Nor savage peering round a tree
  Could chill the blood of such as he.

At length he heard the distant tramp
Of movers who had left their camp,
  Beyond him in the vale.
He reached it as they moved away,
Yet some beside the camp fire stay
  And listen to his tale :

" How from that fearful fever well,
'Tis needless for me now to tell,
    But where—O, where is she
Who nursed me in that fever's spell,
Whom then I knew not—now too well
    She's fondly known to me ?"

Then sobbing spoke the boy of ten,
"She sleeps here in this mountain glen
    Within yon mountain side.
Fever and grief hath racked her brain
Since father died, and she in pain
    Watched at your sick bed side—
And I upon my father's grave.
She sought me, heard your feverish rave,
And strove with all her heart to save,
    But death has claimed his bride."

" No, God forbid !" he said, and hid
His face within his hands.   "O! bid
    My soul deny its truth,
O say that God hath quenched the sun
And caused all streams to backward run,
    Made wrinkled age as youth.
Hath cursed the flowers that sweetest bloom,
Turned sunlight into mid night gloom,
But say not she rests in the tomb
    My soul will curse its truth."

Then spoke again the boy of ten.
" Three days we camped within the glen,
Two days she had no pulse, and then
    They said that she was dead.
Those days we sat beside her form
And O! I thought her heart was warm
    And many tears I shed.
At length I saw them take a spade
And mark off where she should be laid
    Within the dismal ground.

" Then I arose—besought—forbade
That if a grave must, should be made
    A better could be found.
What, lay her in the dark cold clay
Where wolves may dig, and worms may prey?
    Heaven save us from this fault

" But in the solid mountain's side
Like ancients burried those who died
With pick and spade there fashion wide
    A deep and solid vault.
They listened and at last they tried
And dug a grave all deep and wide
    Within the solid rock.
And there they placed her coffin lone
Deep in the solid heart of stone
    That tempests could not shock.

They fitted in its mouth a block,
And then upon its door of rock
They carved in letters rude and plain
The simple words of ' *Ethel Vane.*'

" She dying said that death was gain
The grave would bring a sweeter pain
    Than any earth could give.
That here the weary heart would rove
But love would bloom in bliss above
    Where loving souls could live.

" O sir ! we some times judge amiss
    And reason not as do the wise
Who think upon the spirits bliss
    In its bright home beyond the skies.
For when we look on those who've died,
    Robed in white garments for the tomb,
They should seem as a lonely bride
    When first she wears the orange bloom ;
Unfettered from the ills of strife,
Wed unto life, eternal life."

Then thrice the horseman slacked the rein,
Thrice bowed him to his chargers mane
    With fixed and vacant eye.
Then rousing from his dream again
Too deeply stunned to feel his pain

He threw himself upon the earth
And bid them all "Go forth, go forth,
  Go leave me here to die."

The sun sloped o'er the western hills
  And threw his golden glare
Where Truman Gray in sorrow spills
  His earnest soul in prayer.
He said, "O mountains bow your head;
  O sky bend down and answer now,
Where shall I find my loved—my lost,
  Where hide this throbbing, aching brow?

"I ask of thee all seeing sun,
Where e'er thy mighty orbits run,
Where worlds on worlds crowd on thy sight
Like insects in the summer light.
From this lone star all tempest-tossed,
Where dwells my sweet, my loved, my lost?

"Ye stars! ye constellations bright!
God's worlds of beauty and of light,
  O! tell me if your peerless spheres
Contain an angel robed in white
  Free from all sorrow, and all tears,
That I shall fold unto my breast—
And in eternity be blest?
O Ethel! Shall we meet again
Beyond all sorrow, toil and pain.

In joy, in fadeless beauty meet?
No thorny paths for weary feet,
But thou my gladsome angel sweet?

" I've asked it of the rolling years
    That sweep like torrents to the sea ;
I've asked it of man's hopes and fears
    That reach far o'er eternity.
I've asked it of the mighty God
That plants sweet flowers upon the sod ;
I've asked this of the blooming trees,
The spring, the green grass and the breeze.
If they shall bless each summer day,
Shall human flowers more fair than they
Bloom but to perish and decay ?
If they but bloomed that death might cull,
Why didst thou make them beautiful ?"

The sun sank lower in the West,
The evening star advanced her crest.
He pressed his brow, he bowed his head,
Then, looking to the sky, he said :
" Methought the sun in crimson dyed,
Methought the eternal stars replied :
' Beyond, where Time her billows roll,
The sum and essence of the soul
Shall still exist—live and be blest—
God's chosen ones—God's honored guest ;

And there thou shalt thy love enfold
In perfect bliss, while ages roll.
Else why such longings wrapt in sod—
Else why?   The soul is part of God.
That it should live a thousand years
Beyond all time—free from all tears—
Is it a greater mystery, say,
Than to be born and live one day?'

" God spake.   His words were suns and worlds
    That rolled like chariot wheels in flight,
And, on their trackless path, unfurled
    Their banners, dipped in fadeless light.
He shaped a form of earthly clay
And breathed upon it.   And the ray
He kindled was immortal life—
To dwell awhile 'mid earthly strife;
Then, soaring heavenward. take its flight
Through those vast worlds of fadeless light.
The dragon—Death—spread forth his wings
    And threw a shadow o'er its day :
But, like the flash the lightning brings.
    It sped upon its starry way.

" Yes. Ethel, we shall meet again—
    Where islands slumber in the sea,
And streams of life make glad the plain—
    In the gardens of eternity :

Where flowers of fragrant beauty bloom.
Nor time can blast, nor death consume.
Pile up your walls of massive speech—
　Your granite logic—tier on tier.
Hedge in the soul—ye skeptics teach
　This house of clay prescribes its sphere.
That you can reason and reply,
Is proof the soul can never die.
To think, is to live on—to be,
To love is immortality.
For safe within the pearly gates,
Love's lost jewel shining waits;
Folded hands on pulseless breast
Is but the casket laid at rest."

And now more calmly doth he rise,
And bending strong a rock doth prize
　From out the mountain side—
From out the grave that they had made,
Hewn in the rock with pick and spade—
He enters now.　The coffin lid
He lifts from o'er the form it hid.
　And now the golden tide,
From out the windows of the sun
Falls on the lovely face of one
　Who seems a sleeping bride.
The living pressed the seeming dead,
Threw back the ringlets of her head

And kissed her marble brow,
And said : "O, heart to heart may give
A thrill, to cause the dead to live,
  And heaven may answer now.

"Sure love may enter even graves—
All things are fair, all things are pure,
And naught of evil e'er can lure
  The heart that seeks and saves.
They said her pulse was still, was still—
It seems I feel the slightest thrill."
He placed his hand above her heart,
Then, with a glad and sudden start
  He said: "She lives! she lives!"
Then, on her lips he pressed a kiss,
  Their silence to unseal,
As if he thought love's thrill of bliss
  Could cause death's self to feel,
And steal away that dreamless sleep
Where love can neither smile nor weep.

He chaffed her dimpled ivory hands
  And warmed her marble brow,
And tried to start again life's sands,
  So feebly starting now.
"What is it, I ask of thee, O, death!
  And what O, heaven above,
But a soul brought back from the gates of death
  And a woman's wonderous love?"

He raised her in his arms and wept,
And, from the death-like trance she slept
  He tried to kindle life.
And in his arms with silent tear,
He bore her to the camp fire near
  And stirred it into life.
There wrapt her in some blankets warm,
And bowed above her breathless form.
The sunset gold streamed from the sky,
The laughing brook, stole softly by
  As if it was a solemn thing
For man to love, or maid to die.

*   *   *   *   *   *   *   *   *

At length he placed her on his steed,
And mounting, in his arms with speed
He bore her westward o'er the plain,
And ere the dawn they reached the train.

CANTO TWENTIETH.

MOUNTAIN MEADOW MASSACRE.

On Utah's vales the sun had set,
  Draped in her golden shrouds;
The moon strode through the tangled net
  Of bright and silvery clouds,
And lit the jeweled helmet spread
Above the silent hills, and shed
Refulgent glory o'er their head:
And dipped the mountain-tops in white—
As fair as morn, as still as night.
  The dimpled waves of Great Salt Lake,
Beneath the moonbeams play;
  And southward shone fair Utah Lake,
And southward Mountain Meadow lay.

The rugged hights of Wasatach
  Looked, through the shadows, pale,
To where the gleam of camp-fires flash,
  In Mountain Meadow vale;
And warriors grim, of sable hue,
Talked by the fires in groups of few—

It was a grim and motley sight—
Of Indian, Archee and Danite.
Ill suited it, those groups, to tell
How they attacked, like demons fell,
That train now camped in strong corral—
    That, traveling to the land of gold.
Had sought the Southern Pass,
    To save them from the winter's cold—
To find their graves, alas!

How they approached through the ravine
    And drove their stock away;
And in their ambush, and unseen,
    Fired on the train at break of day.
A dozen fell beneath that fire,
    Which roused the emigrants' stern ire.
They chained their wagons each to each—
    They ditched and fortified with care—
They drew their rifles of long reach
    And fought, strong armed, with bosoms bare.

Ill-fared they, then, the lurking foe—
    Their fierce attack was vain—
For stalwart men hurled back the blow
    And thinned their ranks with slain.
The bullets flew—the bullets slew—
From frontier marksmen, strong and true ;
They scatter, form their ranks anew
'Till backward hurled and routed, too.

The emigrants have won the day,
   The foe hide on the hilly hight ;
And now besiege and guard the way,
   And fear to join the deadly fight
'Gainst those that battle for the right—
   'Gainst arms nerved by the desperate will
To sell their lives most dear,
   And guard their wives and children still,
Through every danger, strife and fear.

Five days besiege. At length the foe
   Conceive the dark design,
By treachery, to lay them low—
   And cruelty, condign.
For. having fought from day to day,
And turned repulsed from every fray,
These Mormon saints and savage fiends,
Thus allied for dark, murderous ends,
Deemed treachery gave the only art
To crush these men of valiant heart.

So, dropping their dark, Indian guise,
Haight, Lee, and others on this wise,
Advance. The emigrants now see
A wagon with a flag of white
And white men, whom they hail with glee.
And lift a girl. all dressed in white,
And signal to draw near—alight.

For on that Mead, five miles by two,
They knew naught but a savage foe;
And, unsuspecting, gladly lend
Consent to meet as friend with friend.

Think ye, e'er on the boundless plain,
    Beat hearts more gladly wildly than they,
Unloaded from dark dread and pain,
    As the besieged, that hour and day
They saw the friendly whites appear,
And welcomed them with lusty cheer?

    For, in the heart of mountains wild,
They had no transportation there—
    Their cattle gone, and danger piled
Her billows o'er their hearts of care.
These sainted fiends, with honied smile,
    Say, "They, as friends, have come to save
The emigrants from savage guile,
    And snatch them from a bloody grave.

" The savages are fierce and strong,
    But, if they'll give up arms and train
And trust *them, they* will right the wrong,
    And see that none—not one—are slain;
And guard them to the towns near by,
Where Mormons rule and none shall die.
They'd have the Indians spare their lives,
Nor harm their children nor their wives."

And they consent.   It best did seem.
    Unarmed, they gather on the green—
With gladsome steps did go—
    While in that Mormon guard, is seen
Their former lurking foe.

Some yards they march when with a yell,
Like fiends who knew their work too well,
Their guard turn on these unarmed men,
And slay them like fat beeves in pen.
And rifles blaze and bullets hail,
And fearful echoes shake the vale.
They shoot, they slay, they strew the way
With brave as ever joined the fray.
No time to seek, no quarter given,
The knife and tomahawk are driven
Through flesh and limb, through heart and brain,
And thus this noble band were slain.
Heavens! what a fearful slaughter then;
Foul murder of brave helpless men;
Wet with their blood the heather waves,
And gory were their nameless graves.
While forward in the captive train,
Their anguished wives behold them slain.
And shrieks and groans of wild despair,
Are borne upon the maddened air.
The guards now turn on youths and wives—
Inhuman slaughter none survives.

18

Behold ! back in the startled train
    Young Truman gaze and fondly bow,
In all the anguish of his pain.
    Above a lovely form that now
Seemed waking from a dream.
She woke, yet seemed to think perchance
That still she dreamed, for with a glance
She partly rose ; she sighed ; she smiled,
And shuddered at the shrieks so wild,
    That now alarmed her ears.
When Truman saw her troubled smile,
He soothed her like a petted child,
    And tried to still her fears
" Ethel ! " he said, " four weeks to-day,
They laid you in the tomb away,
    Believing you were dead.

" I sought you, bore you all alone
From tomb within that heart of stone,
    Where they had made your bed.
I reached the train, all now is plain—
'Tis Indian war, I can't remain.
I fear their guile, now rest awhile,
I will return," and with a smile
He seized his rifle, strode away,
To come no more upon that day.

When he had left her presence, lo !
Burst on his sight the slaughtering foe.

Who now commenced to whet their steel,
On women praying as they kneel.
While from the train rolled fast and wide,
The savage yell and gory tide.
Then Truman's rifle pointed well—
Each flash a distant savage fell.
Beside him stood the boy of ten,
And fought as brave and coolly then.

When others sought the open plain;
  All guarded by the treacherous foe.
They with fair Ethel did remain.
  Who convalescing slow.
Her consciousness did scarcely gain,
  'Till startled by those shrieks of woe.
She 'woke a deeper grief to know.

She 'woke to hear the welkin ring:
The rifles crack. the bullet sing;
The shriek of wives; the clash of knives;
The death groan of a hundred lives.
To catch her lover's words and smile.
Then tremble at the dangers wild,
That wrapt as fire a funeral pile.

Then Truman and the boy of ten.
Fought well and nobly, but no pen
Can paint the slaughter fierce the while
Of savage rage and Mormon guile :

Or Truman's anguish when he saw
No courage known to human law—
No feat of strength or daring brave,
From slaughter's tide could hope to save
    The woman that he loved.
When closely pressed the dastard foe,
He clubbed his rifle, at each blow
He hewed a pathway wide before,
    And well his courage proved.
But courage now availed him naught,
To save the train or her he sought.
Pressed backward by the gory wave,
He deemed it best his life to save ;
Not rash in folly's useless strife,
To end the faded hopes of life.

He and the boy with nimble feet,
Through a dark ravine found retreat,
And while fierce pillage rolled her tide,
They sought and reached the mountain side.
And covering well their winding trail,
They wandered on through mount and vale :
For days and weeks still journeyed far,
Until they reached a fort of war.
There told their tale of dangers wild ;
Of Indian rage. and Mormon guile.
'Twas doubted then, but since proved true,
That Brigham of the slaughter knew—

Ordered attack, and then did share
The lion's part of booty there.
This monster saint smiled on the deed
Of crime, that made the Gentiles bleed.

The sun all-seeing, whose bright eye
   Lights up the universe of time,
Turned black as Erebus, would die
   At sight of such incarnate crime,
But that the future holds for these,
   Beyond their brief, accurs'd probation,
A torment, wide and deep as seas,
   And seven-fold hot with red perdition.
But for the antidote to come,
   The very worlds would stand aghast,
And maddened angels, with swift tread,
   Unbar the gates of all the past
And leap the chasm of all wrath,
   To shatter vengeance on their head.

If retribution these shall miss—
   If good and bad that sink to dust
Must tread alike the realms of bliss :
   If monsters of such crime and lust
Must with the righteous join their song
   Or sleep alike the eternal night :
Where, then, is Justice ? Here's a wrong
   The power of God could not make right.

Retribution—hurt whom it may—
Is part of Justice and God's sway—
The fitness of eternal things;
'Tis Truth well armed, and Law on wings.
Say it is not—and Reason's mad,
And you abolish good and bad.

The lovers thus were parted far,
While Hope seemed as a fading star
    That soon—too soon, must set.
Yet sickness, death and carnage spared
The life of her who all these shared—
    In beauty lingering yet.
For where she shone rude discord ceased,
And smiled—her beauty carried peace.
Her very weakness proved a shield;
Ere turned that horde from carnage field,
    The Indian Agent, Hamlin, came.

Her voice, her beauty charmed him so
He vowed to shield from harm and woe—
    Her safety at all hazard claim.
And thus he spoke, and raised his brand:
" Her life—her safety I demand.
No Mormon stands more true than I ;
Who harms her by this sword shall die."

His word was law to red men there ;
    They feared him, and fell back in haste ;

Not so a Danite with long hair,
  Strode on and said, " No words to waste
Where this ' avenging angel' sweeps,"
And bounded forward at two leaps.
Hamlin disdained to use his steel,
  But caught him with a grip like vise
And crushed his head against a wheel
  As one would crush a shell of ice.

Another came his sword to thrust—
He shivered it like bits of dust,
And ground his breast beneath his heel
And pinned it there with pointed steel.
" Stand back! Beware! for he will find
' Who enters here leaves hope behind.' "

" Though I be Mormon, ye may fear
The Government that sends me here.
One word from me, and you may stand
More cursed than is yon slaughtered band,
But grant me this, and none shall need
To know from me your murderous deed."
He stood there like a frowning tower,
And crushed them with his words of power.
He emphasized each word he spoke
With sword guard and a ponderous stroke
On axle tire, and at the last,
He ground it like to bits of glass

Beneath his hand.   With strength to dare
Dead at his feet and forehead bare,
He scowled like lion fierce at bay,
And held them till he had his way,
Soon had her borne in haste with care
Unto his house, some miles from there,
When well, in secret sent her home,
Where she arrived no more to roam.

CANTO TWENTY-FIRST.

THE SPANISH MAID—AN EPISODE.

On California's golden strand,
Where proud Pacific skirts the land,
Where once a mining town had stood
A city 'rose in bustling mood,
And costly mansions did appear
Along a mountain streamlet clear ;
While cottages, a cheerful sight,
Befront the streets in rows of white.
And order reigned and social life,
Where once was scenes of rudest strife.

There in a cottage neat and fair,
Together sat an aged pair :
An aged Spaniard and his spouse,
Whose heads were white, whose forms were bowed,
And on whose face of wrinkled care
A shade of sorrow lingered.   There
They sat in silence—feeble, old,
Before a grate of slumbering coal
Whose flickering shades of light and gloom
Spread o'er the dimly lighted room.

While hanging o'er the mantle rare,
Was picture of a maiden fair—
Dark, melting eyes, with dreamy grace,
Set off a lovely, lustrous face
And placid brow, where sable braid,
In dark and glossy folds were laid.

"Twas twilight.   On the hills afar
The night advanced her sable car,
And o'er the sky of darkening blue
The dusky shadows grew, and grew :
While, through the shadows might be seen,
A fair-haired man with business mien
Advancing to the cottage—where
He ope'd the door and entered.   There,
When all were seated, and a light
Dispelled the shadows of the night—
And, when the smouldering fire was fed,
One of the aged couple said :
" Well, Señor ; we are growing old
And soon may die ; so we were told
To have a lawyer write our will—
Though we've no heirs—yet still—yet still,
The thought does make my old eyes fill—
We once did have a fair young girl
With rosy face. and glossy curl,
That romped and played with gladsome glee—
Light of our home, but now ah, me !

We're old, and lonely as you see,
No child to cheer our aged years,
No comfort but in silent tears:
But hence to go, nor leave behind
Descendant of our name and kind."

And then she wept, till, to her aid
The old man came, and sadly said :
"She was our angel in her glee,
In childhood oft she climbed my knee,
And talked, and smiled bewitchingly
At morning's dawn, and evening's close ;
And grew in beauty like the rose,
Fair as the morn at early dawn,
Fair as the lillies on the lawn ;
But one bright morn she disappeared,
Nor aught of her since then we heard.

I thought, that eve she kissed good night,
That tears gleamed in her eyelids bright,
And tears streamed through each tender word—
Her voice shook as I ne'er had heard.
I would not judge her harsh—unfair,
Though 'silver threads' are in my hair
That was most glossy black, the day
We 'rose and found her gone away ;
And yet I've thought—the thought I've cursed—
That she fled with a youth she nursed,

Who, by the robbers, left for dead,
She tended long at his sick bed.
We *will* her all our large estate:
One-third to him who learns her fate
And then restores her to her own.
So write the will; our will is known."
Earl Darring heard, and wrote with skill,
Signed, witnessed. 'twas a legal will.

And, when the business all was o'er,
Earl Darring said: "Three years ago
I met a friend upon the plain,
Who telling o'er his griefs again,
Spoke of a fair Castillian maid;
Who and himself were captives made,
Who nursed him, and who, at the stake,
Still strived to save him for love's sake.

I think it is of her you speak,
And for her I will search and seek
And naught will spare, till I declare
If dead, or lives your daughter fair?"
The old folks wept, and thanked him o'er,
Until they parted at the door.

  * * * * * *

Months after this, Earl Darring rode
Along a dreary mountain road,

And urged his steed fleet as he could
Through a dark Oregonian wood,
The night approached—a storm was nigh,
While, raging in the distant sky,
The roaring thunders crash and peal
Till, through their ribs of rock and steel,
The hills and valleys seem to feel,
And every leaflet on the tree
To tremble with fear's agony ;
And all the forest monarchs bowed
Unto the thunder and the cloud.

Still onward came the driving storm
That bent Earl Darring's graceful form,
And snapped and tossed the forest trees,
Like leaflets borne upon the breeze.
As on he rode, with fearful force,
Their limbs were scattered in his course,
Till through the forest—little trod,
He lost all traces of the road ;
Still onward pressed through wilds unknown,
Till night began to lower down.
When. through the storm, he heard with fear,
Pursuing hoof falls drawing near—
And turning, soon did wondering spy
A lady. mounted. gallop nigh.

She rode erect. with graceful form,
And seemed unconscious of the storm :

With cheeks flushed at the grandeur's scene,
And flowing hair of sable sheen,
She seemed Diana—huntress queen.
Her mien, her hair—unbound by hood—
Made her seem goddess of the wood,
Nymph. fearless of all earthly harm,
And empress of the raging storm.
As she, approaching, galloped nigh,
A tree-top, waving far on high,
Came crashing down.   Ere he could heed,
It brushed Earl Darring from his steed
And laid him, stunned, upon the ground
Beneath its weight—that held him down.

Almost as quick as could be seen
She cleared the open space between,
Dismounted, and then Earl released,
And helped him on his waiting beast.
He seemed amazed to thus behold
A dark-eyed beauty brave and bold
Assist him, and bind up his head,
As gay and fearless thus she said,
" What pity such a glorious storm
So grand to see, should do you harm.
Such dangers I have often dared,
I've courted death and little cared."
He thanked her with a courteous mien,
And gazed bewildered on this queen.

Her dark-eyed splendor form so rare.
Her horsemanship and features fair
Was so bewitching to his eye
He scarce could frame a wise reply.

The path was wild, the way unknown
But to his heroine guide alone:
She bade him follow; then for miles
They galloped through the woodland wilds,
Then halting as night's curtains fell;
She said: "Just yonder in that dell
The Indians in their wigwams dwell
There long detained a captive, I
Oft wished release, or wished to die,
But ne'er have learned the distant way
To where the towns and cities lay.

"And long they've watched and spared my life
For ransom, or a Chieftains wife.
In distant wars the braves from home
I am more privileged to roam.

" But stranger list, heed what you hear,
If life and freedom's valued dear
Conceal yourself here in this wood,
And I will bring you needed food
At early dawn.   Here rest till then
Concealed from worse than savage men."

" A world of thanks fair, noble friend
Heaven doth her fairest angel send
To guide me through these unknown ways,
Else should I perish.   Coming days
Shall claim from me thy grateful praise."
Scarce ere this gallant speech was made
She vanished through the woodland shade.
Then soon exhausted nature sought
The sweet oblivion Morpheus brought ;
While in his dreams of storms that blew
He saw an angel looking through.
At dawn of day 'rose soft and clear
This music on the atmosphere.

SONG.

Only a dark-eyed maid was she,
Listing to love's wild melody ;
Treading the stairs to the golden sun,
Where the soul will trust 'till the soul's undone ;
Dreaming the golden dream "he's mine "
"Till the heart glows " warm as a world of wine."

Softly she laughed in her witching glee ;
Sweetly she dreamed " I am free, I am free."
She knew not the song the wild birds feel,
She knew not the chain and its links of steel ;
She knew but to list where his footsteps tread,
And tremble with joy at words he said.

He won the heart that was pure and true ;
He won the heart, and he broke it too.
And now the heart once glad and free,
Sighs to the wild wood's minstrelsy.
And though the wild woods know it not,
That longing heart hath ne'er forgot.

She paused.   Earl quickly rising, sees
Her slow approaching through the trees.
She bade good morn, and did alight,
Then said, " Here's food for strength and flight,"
Then speaking thus he scanned her face,
" I long have sought from place to place,
A maid of fair Castillian race.
Long years ago she left her home,
And still continues far to roam.
That she was captured some avow :
Her aged parents seek her now."

Then she replied. "'Tis her you see :
I hoped they ne'er had grieved for me—
I wished no eye, not Heaven's above,
To scan the mystery of my love.
I wished like ship upon the wave,
To sink where none could see or save,
And not a bubble reach the shore.
From where I sank to rise no more.
And that the heart so wild untamed,
That I have cursed, and some have blamed.

Might moulder back to whence it came,
Unwept, unknown, without a name.
Far from my kindred and my kind,
I'd track the mysteries of the mind:
And build a palace in my scorn,
Upon the golden gates of morn;
Bedeck it with the jeweled stars,
And with the rainbow's spangled bars.

" There lift the curtain of the skies,
And bid eternal visions rise;
Trace through the essence of the soul,
My being back to God, the whole—
As from a seed, the forests trace.
So from this soul, the worlds of space,
And up and onward till I find
The endless universe of mind.
But, as a wounded, suffering dove,
I'd shun the ways of trust and love—
I'd ask of God who what thou art,
And what this mystery in my heart.

" I'd scorn an angel from above
If it but whispered, ' love! love! '
I'd write upon the zenith sky
A blazing song of that proud lie—
As brilliant as the crimson stars,
As dreadful as the clash of wars.

I'd pin it to the nightly moon,
And to the dazzling sun at noon.
I'd send it crashing through the brain
Till every trusting fool was slain.
I once was queen of fairy isles
Where castles rose like diamond piles,
That glittered in the golden sun,
Where silver streams to music run,
And knights were gay and hearts were won.

" But now those isles are barren rocks,
That breast the storm and bear its shock.
I've scanned the fabric of this world,
The gauzy banners hope unfurl'd.
Its wares and merchandise I brand
Accursed, as the drifting sand
Upon Sahara's scorching plain —
But meant to blight and curse with pain.

" I lift my hand to God on high,
And brand Earth a stupendous lie—
Where souls are cursed by blights of time
And hearts must shrivel in their prime.
Great God, 'tis not the world for me —
Hand down a world from sorrow free,
Where life is one perennial bloom,
And hearts ne'er shudder at the tomb;
Where love flows out, and joy flows in,
And souls ne'er dream of death or sin—

Not like this life-path martyrs trod.
Traced by the blood-tracks on the sod.

" I'd rather dwell in forests wild,
Tracked only by the forest child ;
Far trom the haunts of men, alone —
A hermit, in a hut of stone;
Far from ambition. love or fear,
Unknown to sympathetic tear—
Than, having loved, to be despised,
Or, trusting. prove that trust unwise."

Then spoke Earl Darring : " But to day
I deemed you gayest of the gay.
Your thoughts and actions ill accord,
I dreamt your heart ne'er knew a lord.
Our lives have held an equal fate—
Both trusting early suffer late.
But what of that ?   To truly love
Ne'er soiled the plumage of a dove,
Ne'er made a madman or a fiend,
But raised us to the angel kind,
Who tread the courts of bliss above.
Whose every thought is winged with love.

" For God carves on each leaf of time
Love, as a poem, grand, sublime.
Go read it, for it is the soul
Of Him who did creation roll

Upon the endless shoreless sea
Of space and God's eternity.
Who seeks will find that heaven above
Is but the joy of sinless love.
Then seek it in the world below.
The rarest gift earth can bestow ;
A foretaste of the heavenly bliss.
The only Eden found on this
Encrusted orb of rock and steel,
Whose torn and cracked ribs deeply feel
The raging fires beneath its crest,
Like untamed passion in the breast.
To curb these fires with wise control
Is heaven's command unto the soul.
Yet nature's impulse must have vent,
Or earthquakes rend its firmament.

From heaven's wisdom this we draw
Love is fulfillment of the law.
And they see but perfection's rise,
Who look through loves sweet-beaming eyes.
Why, with bold pride and haughty scorn,
A warrior once to empire born
Threw back a world of crowns like this
For Cleopatra's rapturing kiss.
Even Hercules took humble seat,
And spun at fair Omphales' feet :
Lysander, for sweet Hero's glance,
Oft braved the sea waves' dark expanse."

" Yes," she replied, " some dupes have sighed,
And some blown out their brains and died,
On thoughtful men of judgment cool,
Oft love has nobly written, ' fool !'
And minds who've weighed the sun and stars
Been prisoned by its silken bars.

" I must suppose, on this earth's crest
All feel it beating 'neath their vest.
It is an old complaint, they say,
That Adam had it in his day,
And swapt his Paradise, the simple,
For Mrs. Eve, and a bite of apple.

"They say men, honored. great and true,
Philosophers, and parsons, too,
Men of brave actions, courage worth.
Men who've subdued the mighty earth,
Done all the great things 'neath the stars,
Have felt their hearts beat 'neath its bars
Like some poor wounded fluttering dove,
When pierced by Cupid's dart of love ;
Have dwelt with sweet, ecstatic bliss
On woman's form and 'rapturing kiss."

He said : " Scoff not—rebuke man's wrong,
But not the tie that makes him strong.
Love never made our manhoods weak,
'Tis strength to dare, 'tis heaven to seek.

If eagle eye will quail before
And voices strong as battle's roar
Sink trembling soft as maiden's sigh
At sight of a soft beaming eye :
If spirits like the setting sun,
Begirt with glories they have won,
Who've mastered all the arts of time,
Strong armed as giants in their prime :
Have blanched at sight of woman's face
With its bright loveliness and grace :
'Tis homage to her nature due—
And manhood's highest honor too.

" This homage makes fond man to wield
The ax in groves, the plow in field
And belt the earth with iron bands
To gather products of all lands.
And fret the bosom of the seas
With millions of rich argosies :
To win her love, and earn her praise.
And bless her in a thousand ways.

"And say not to the God on high
Earth is a grand stupendous lie.
Earth is our mother, from her clay
Were made the forms we praise each day.
And when the shores of death are pressed,
Within her bosom we must rest.

'Tis man hath wrinkled earth's sad brow,
She once was heaven, what is she now?
The gentle mists bedewed her o'er,
Where storms now beat and tempests roar.
Once fruit and flowers spontaneous grew,
And skies were one soft vail of blue;
Now man must force earth with the plow,
And live by toil and sweat of brow.
Yet by his soul-power he hath won,
Some honor 'neath the circling sun :
Yet soul discards, and makes his goal,
Heaven for the body, not the soul."

She spoke, "This truth should well be known,
Man does not live by bread alone :
But truly lives by wisdom's light :
By knowledge, truth and love of right ;
By honest worth and will to try :
By beauties of the earth and sky ;
By soul developed, strong and free :
By works of faith, love, charity :
And I can most admire the man,
Who takes these in, as heaven's blue span
Takes in the stars, and holds them there.
Strong as the night in silent prayer."

Then he, "Such souls are strong and feel
Within the ring of clear blue steel :

Like mailed warriors came and went,
And worlds bowed to their strong intent.
There have been spirits who have trod.
The earth and towered like a god;
Have walked amid the stars like night,
Their brows begirt with beams of light;
Yet love hath made them weak or strong,
As they loved wisely or loved wrong.
Hath dropped into each earnest soul,
Like dews of heaven, or beams of gold,
Or leaping in the heart like fire,
Uncurbed each wild and fierce desire.
And wrapt it like a world on fire.
Hath gained the chariot of the will,
And seized the reins, urged passion till
Truth, honor, sense and wisdom fell,
And plunged them in the lowest hell."

Juanita said, " From pain long past,
Let not remorse dark lingering last;
But let us rear to heaven high,
A wall above the sunset sky
Of faded hopes.   Let Gomorrahs blaze,
God guides us into other ways:
And gives us strength to do and dare,
And bear the ills we can but bear.
Now having breakfast'd, mount your steed,
We've lingered long, and now must speed:

I fear we're watched by Indian spies,
Your steed awaits—time quickly flies."

Scarce on his steed the horseman swung,
When forth an ambushed Indian sprung,
His rifle at Earl Darring raised ; when, lo!
She struck his steed a sudden blow ;
Which jumped just as the Indian shot.
Unhurt they galloped from the spot.

From a rosy morn to a brilliant noon
    Two lovers rode gayly on and on,
In the twilight gray, 'neath a laughing moon
    A new love came like a blushing dawn.

They sighed a sigh, but not for the past,
    For the dreams of youth had vanished away,
And the newest love will grow old at last,
    Each folly must have its own sweet day.

Man can fall in love but once in a life,
    He may feel affection again and again,
But the twilight calm 's too fair for strife,
    And a second love is a sweeter pain.

The soul grows strong when its pride is bitter
    And the heart is mellowed by grief and pain,
And our lives oft prove the wiser and better
    For the things we miss than the things we gain.

And the saddest thing on a dreary earth,
  Is a withered heart and a loveless life :
Where the fires of soul on a cheerless hearth,
Like Marius, brood o'er the ruins of strife.

Though it be as the moon to the bright sunlight,
  A new love is better than sighing,
And to nurse a pale dream in the cold twilight,
  Worse than heart to sweet heart replying.

The picture is bright as a starry night,
  And the things I see, ah. me ! ah. me !
For the hours go round with a fresh delight,
  And the future spreads like a sunset sea.

CANTO TWENTY-SECOND.

THE WEDDING—EDEN REBUILT.

When weeks had passed, and months had rolled,
And Autumn spread her skirts of gold,
And trees assumed their robes of brown
And shook their golden glories down,
Which, ripening in the mellow sun,
Fulfilled fruition Spring begun:
All bounteous nature's wise employ
Now gladdening every sense with joy;
While in the twilight of the year
The full earth swells with silent cheer;
And o'er the Autumn skies unfold
Rich, hazy mists of yellow gold:
When woods in many hues are dressed,
And soft contentment fills the breasts
Of feathered songsters in the grove,
And human hearts that sigh with love.

Just at the close of Autumn day,
Mid dusky shadows dim and gray,
As Autumn moon brim full of gold
Rose laughing o'er the hill tops bold;

Before a mansion bright with lights
A carriage stops, a man alights,
And Truman Gray is at the door
Of Hugh McVeigh, and on the floor
Two friends of old have grasped the hand,
And pausing, gaze, and gazing stand.
The parlors, all aglow with light,
Are gay with wealth and fashion bright,
And women fair, in rich attire,
And men that gaze, and oft admire,
In bright confusion come and go
As like a glittering stream they flow ;
For wealth had come with jeweled hand
To give a welcome proud and grand
Where Truman, at his journey's end,
Had grasped the hand of truest friend.

But ere he to the parlors passed
He said, "so many years have cast
Their shadows o'er the life that's past
Since I have grasped that hand so true,
And gazed into those eyes of blue ;
I must gaze on that form again,
And kiss from cheeks the last tear stain."
Then to a quiet parlor, they
Did quickly wend their anxious way,
Where soon, in radiant beauty rare,
Came Ethel Vane, all smiling fair.

Maturity had touched the lines
In face and form, that oft refines,
Like fruit that's felt the summer sun
Till luscious ripeness hath begun.

Nor brush can paint, nor chisel trace
The mould of form or lines of face,
The brow of white or breast of snow,
The cheeks that smile or eyes that glow,
The beam of soul, the swell of breast,
The tint of lips that love hath pressed,
The glossy gleam of soft brown hair,
The queenly mould of shoulders fair,
The plump, soft hands of ivory pale,
Fair as twin lillies of the vale,
With dimples laughing on the cheek
Where Cupid plays his hide and seek,
The dainty foot, the fairy tread.
The regal toss of shapely head.

A Juno, fair, with queenly air.
A Hebe in form, Diana fair,
A Venus smiling rich, with joy.
A Helen ere she wept a Troy,
Beatrice Cenci's charming grace,
With smile of heaven upon her face.
A nymph, a goddess who had fed
On nectar sweets, ambrosia bread

Had ne'er been crowned by gods a queen
More fair.   More fair was never seen.

Oh! loveliness and beauty fair!
If loveliness and beauty rare
Is found beneath the vault of blue,
Beneath the stars of golden hue,
Beneath the dazzling orb of day,
Or pallid white moon's silvery ray,
Upon the earth of checkered green,
Or in the ships that sail between,
Or in the isles of sunny seas,
'Mid summer climes and balmy breeze;
That loveliness so fair, and pure,
That doth man's heart beguile and lure—
Above all objects, old or new,
Is woman—noble, lovely, true.

In all the edens here below—
If earth again can eden know—
The brightest charm and sweetest bliss
Of heaven on earth, is found in this:
To clasp to manly breast that's true
A loving breast that's warm and pure,
Gaze in soft eyes of heavenly blue
And kiss from lips the honey due.
Be circled in the ivory pale
Of dimpled arms, where joy can sail.

Ah, Comte! Well thy followers knew
To whom of earth was worship due,
While reasoning out of earth and air
All spirits and all angels fair,
The Bible, and the thought of God—
Thee as the lovliest on earth's sod
They met, agreed to meet each week
To worship, and thy praises speak.

And France with all her polished art
More famed for culture, than for heart,
Abolished by one wild decree
The sacred Book and Deity.
Yet, knowing man would love, adore,
Placed woman where God stood before.

They met, one bends with loving grace,
And one lifts up a smiling face
And soft soul-beaming eyes, as one
Would lift her soul up to the sun.
They press the hand and touch the lip
For love is sweet and love will sip
And taste the nectar and the wine,
Or droop in sadness and repine.
For thus it has, since Adam tried
Forbidden fruit, and round him tied
The fig-leaf apron.   Art began
To throw around the fallen man

A mantle that might nature hide.
Though nature knows she is belied."

" My love," he said, " The years gone by
Have stole no luster from thine eye,
And time but adds a softer grace
To lines of beauty on thy face.
The tinge of sadness on thy brow
Hath caught angelic brightness now.
And in those orbs of love that roll
I catch sweet glimpses of the soul.
And syren song could ne'er beguile
A wanderer like thy gladsome smile.
Since here I've held thee to my breast
My heart hath lost its long unrest.
One moments bliss hath swept away
The pain of many a stormy day.
Since I am thus so fondly blest
What love, is now thy dear behest ?
Dost wish to dwell upon a throne
Or tread all paths that fame hath known,
Or wander where soft sunlight falls
On verdant bowers and palace walls ?

" Or." " Hush ! hush !" she said ; " You should not
     tease,
I'd ask a richer boon than these—
That sweeter, brighter charm doth bring
Than gilded trappings of a king—

Than sceptered empire e'er unfurled
Or conquest of a changling world.

Two hearts beside a cheerful hearth,
And I the best beloved of earth:
The best beloved the sun hath seen,
Or treads the earth of living green,
And, in the future paths unknown,
No more to walk life's ways alone,
One at my side my path to cheer,
And smile away each gloomy fear;
To feel one heart, all, all my own,
Ah! this were better than a throne.
The flag of conquest then I'd furl,
One heart should be my sceptered world."

"A woman's wish, but granted ere
Thy words had fallen on my ear;
Thou art my empress, unto thee
My soul hath wed its fealty:
My heart shall own thy regal sway,
And deem it perfect as the day.
And guard thee in its sheen of light.
From heat of noon and gloom of night,
Thy guardian spirit shall it be.
And guard thee as the cliffs the sea,
I'll crown thy brow with Love's pure kiss,
And print thy lips with gems like this."

O! very sweet, indeed, to some,
Does love with its beguilings come,
When those who've wandered far and wide
May sit together side by side,
'Neath fairest bowers of earthly bliss,
To dream the lover's dream of bliss;
But sacred is true lovers' joy,
Nor eye should view, nor pen should toy,
To gaze too free is to destroy.

When two swift, fleeting hours had passed,
They rose and to bright parlors passed,
And ere that joyous eve was o'er,
Three stood upon the " tufted floor,"
The man of God, and those bright two—
One strong, one fair, both tried and true.
And there they pledged their changeless truth,
Through time, till death, that nothing ruth
Should ever change or blast its truth ;
And when the proud " I do " was said,
The man of God bowed low his head,
And lifted up his voice in prayer,
That blessings rich fall on that pair.

So we will lift in prayer the soul
That highest heaven may be goal,
That rarest joys may shower down,
As rich as gems in sceptered crown.

That they may journey, hand in hand,
Until they reach the heavenly land,
And on eternal hills afar,
Glow with soft love, as glows a star;
Feed on its beams—heaven's rayless light—
And talk of clouds that dimmed the night
Of earthly love; and walk up higher
And warm their souls by heaven's fire—
Unsullied fire of truth and love—
God's soul, that smiles in heaven above.

O! happy hours of wedded bliss!
O! Eden joys in earth like this!
O, heaven—if heaven's beneath the sun—
'Tis Eden home—there is but one.*
And they did make love's honeymoon
Last through all life—then end too soon.
And Truman bought, wherein to dwell,
The loved old home—fair Eden Dell;
And built again the mansion fine,
With porticoes enwreathed with vine.
'Mid joyous scenes and rosy hours,
They walked amid its lovely bowers.

The nearest thing to heaven's dome,
Earth's brightest spot, a lovely home,

* The great statesman, Edmund Burke, bore this testimony to domestic
felicity. He said: "So sweet were the enjoyments of domestic life to him,
that every care vanished the moment he entered beneath his own roof."

Where from the world and its unrest,
The mind at ease. the heart at rest,
Folds wings of love o'er peaceful breast.
And they that often entered there,
Breathed for its peace an earnest prayer,
That all might love so true and well,
All homes be like fair Eden Dell.

For love that stayed, had entered there,
Made it its home and atmosphere;
Not such a place as many share—
A place to growl and frown with care;
Nor such as beasts go when they need
To eat—lie down—rise up and feed;
Nor such as tyrants go—to sway
Despotic power—the Cæsar play—
O'er gentler natures sternly rule—
At home, a lord—abroad, a fool.
Nor where the gentler natures rise
With taunting lip and flashing eyes,
Out-babbling Babel with one tongue.
Till crinoline the scepter's swung.
And to the last, as first, unfurled,
Drives man from Eden to the world.

O, erring man! where'er ye roam.
Turn oft and fondly to thy home:
O, make it what God meant it here—
Life's sweetest boon, love's holy sphere.

At morn, at eve, with loving grace,
Enfold thy loved with glad embrace;
O, kiss away each anxious thought
Of thy fair wife's, and vow that naught
Shall make thee cruel, harsh, unkind.
Enthrone her in thy heart and mind
As God's best angel lent thee here
To bless thy life with loving cheer.

Man seeks distinction, fame and gain,
And glories in ambition's pain,
And toil for wealth his life employs—
These please him like his childhood toys.
His pleasure is more gold, more land,
And love is second in command.
But woman's sphere is less to shine:
Home is her temple and her shrine.
Her heart can neither soar nor sing
Unless love shield it with his wing.
Affection 's with her nature blent,
Her only starry firmament;
Where, roofed within its heavenly span,
Man is her idol.   Faithless man!

In after years, glad Truman learned
Earl Darring wealth and honor earned,
And to his yearning breast did fold
A love, more true than one of old.

Juanita, tossed from mountain side,
Had still survived and was his bride.
Both, weaned from first love, did entwine
As stately oak and graceful vine,
That tossing storms and tempests thrill
But made to cling the closer still.
The boy of ten, O, where and when
Stood forth among brave, stalwart men
An Indian hunter such as he
From eastern to the western sea?
He kept with vengeful steel, and brave,
The vow made on his father's grave.

Beaumont, he wed a wealthy shrew,
Who ran him and their fortunes through;
Till, all unloved, poor and unblest,
He came and went at her behest,
Till joys of life to him were fled
And all its blighted hopes were dead,
Its bliss and sweets to acid turned.
Its worthless fires to ashes burned.
He sought the bowl—and naught could check—
He wanders now—a hopeless wreck.
While Truman claimed, with worthy pride,
That all true lovers, far and wide,
Should earn their gold and win their bride.
And noblest bliss he found in store
For those who, when, love's wanderings o'er,

Proved faithful, and this fact was known—
Each loved each for themselves alone,
And mutual love and faith did share,
That time nor wanderings could impair.

*   *   *   *   *   *

When vesper stars their silver tents
  Pitch on the plains of spangled blue,
And from the starry battlements
  Falls music like the crystal dew,
Two lovers stroll and fondly gaze
  Up to the heavens, as on the day
They caught the pure, celestial blaze,
  Though " silver threads" are 'mong the gray.

The world is old, and hearts are cold,
  And traffic's ships are on the sea,
And men are bold for love and gold,
  And some are false as false can be.
The life they gain 's a stormy main,
  A sobbing, bleak and dreary day.
Let love remain to sweeten pain—
  'Tis bright as heaven's starry way.

WAYWARD FANCIES.

Mark well, who wed should give the hand
With undivided heart, and stand,
In single purpose, true to one ;
Or else the loving soul's undone
  In bitterness and agony.
And like the curse that blights the land,
The heart's at variance with the hand.
A house divided can not stand,
  True love should know no jealousy.

Mark more, brave souls with scorn of pain,
With life's devotion, oft in vain
Have sought with generous faith and true,
Like loyal knights, return well due
  Affections peerless dowry.
Yet sought in vain, and found too late,
It was not there to win, and Fate
Had linked them to a faithless mate,
  They thought the flower of chivalry.

TWO STRANGER GUESTS.

" The sweetest joy, the wildest woe is love,
The taint of earth, the odor of the skies is in it."

" Young man you say that love is best,
   And yet you cannot reason why;
It works dark deeds, and broods unrest,
   And makes the yearning bosom sigh?"
Thus spoke a dark-eyed stern old man,
   And stroked his beard of silver gray;
And watched the stars drift now and then,
   From out the twilight of the day;
As at the magic touch divine,
They formed their cohorts into line,
   And marched upon their nightly way.
'Twas where three sat twixt gloom and light
Beside a camp fire blazing bright;
It chanced as conversation's stream
Rolled on, that love became their theme.

" You say that love will reason not,
   And yet it has a power supreme,
Beyond where reason is forgot,
   And tyrant passion is supreme.

                    And yet you can not reason why
The God who does the things he would,
    And wisdom questions not his will,
Should make the noblest means of good,
    The very instruments of ill?
And man should never love you say,
    Behold this scar above my eye,
'Tas wrought upon an evil day,
                    Its story is my best reply.

" I loved a maiden years ago,
    Back in the sunny days of youth;
    It was a grand, an awful truth,
And yet I never told her so.
Suffice it that we had a quarrel,
    Suffice it that we said good by:
Suffice it that we parted then,
    For she was proud and so was I.
I married one that well I knew,
Was paragon of all that's true.

" She wedded, and we seldom met.
    Some how she thrilled me with her eyes;
I wondered if I loved her yet,
    And then the thought I would despise.
        ' Well what of that, felt she the same?'
I had all love I could have asked.
    And yet it was a something tame;

Beside the love that o'er me flashed,
  I could not help, was I to blame?
When she was near all things were fair,
  I felt new joy swell through my veins;
When she was gone I lacked for air,
  And wandered in my restless pains.

" I'd tasted of the better wine,
  I could not quench my thirst with dew,
I longed to pluck this nectared vine
  And warm my being through and through;
Yet still I trod the narrow way,
And said to Satan day by day :
' Get thou behind me—go thy way.'

" It chanced upon a Summer night
  I strolled beneath a cooling grove;
The moon shone wondrous fair and bright,
  My heart was restless, and would rove.
When lo! I heard a gentle sob
  Near by within a moonlit bower:
It made each pulse of being throb,
  'Twas *she*, heaven bless the joyous hour.
We met; it was a glorious pain
  That bid new tides of feeling roll;
She wept a husband's cold disdain,
  I was a hungry, famished soul.
I took her hand, some words of love

Flowed low and softly in my speech:
She blushed, and fluttered like a dove,
    Until our hearts throbbed each to each
And nestled there in sweeter speech.

    " ' Dora,' I said, 'the years go by,
We are not loved as we could love;
    There's sadness in thy noble eye.
Think'st thou there is a God above?
    What matter that we've vowed a vow,
And others wear the marriage ring;
    What matter, love, is monarch now,
And joy smiles 'neath his rosy wing.
    Could God forbid that we should drink
When pleasure's fountain is in reach,
    Could he forbid that love should link
Her dreams in deeper joy than speech?
    Look down into thy secret soul,
Were we not famished until now?
    Then let us drink our being full,
Love's altar is the place to bow.

    " ' Would'st thou deny, yet tempt the thirst
    When streams of bliss are flowing nigh?
I'd drink, let stoics be accursed,
    If it were death, I'd love to die.
This once, in all the lonely years,
Let our glad hearts pursue their ease,
Affection taste the streams that please;

Drink deep the Samian wine that cheers,
Our souls upon love's nectar feast,
With bliss the boon, and God the priest;
And sailing past all doubtful seas
Wave nature's banner to the breeze—
Love's stronger than man's frail decrees.'

"The moon looked through the silent night
  And smiled so sweetly down:
The golden hours their velvet flight
  Stole o'er the starry crown.
We trod the stars beneath our feet,
  We shamed the bashful moon,
We made the sky our bridal sheet,
  And called the midnight noon.

" The dalliance of that rosy hour
  Was sweetest of life's fleeting dream—
Our souls met in love's magic bower
  And mingled in one stream.
We drank at that perennial spring
  God made in Paradise
To soothe the wily serpent's sting
  Where knowledge should suffice.

" We plucked the very bread of heaven
  From off the table of the gods:
We entered where another Eden
  Blushed through the bloom of rosy sods.

We slaked our thirst and warmed the soul
And felt new tides of being roll.

"'The streams from which we'd drank before
    Had not such power to tempt our thirst;
We wished to taste and taste it o'er
And sail this sea from shore to shore
And drink and die and be no more,
    Let heaven decree the worst.

" The golden hours flew swift and fleet—
    We took no note of honeyed time—
Earth's fair elysian was to sweet;
What starving soul would fear to eat,
    Or question if it were a crime?
O! I could feast forever there
    Upon her beauty as a star
And dream there was no heaven so fair,
    And fear no rude alarms of war.

" But what a waking from a dream !
I heard my loving Dora scream;
    I saw a bright uplifted sword,
And through its sudden flash and gleam
    I knew her angry lord.
I saw the stars—behold the scar !
It was a thrust of more than war,
    And brought a rude alarm.

But mine was more than leopard's leap;
Roused by a sudden blow from sleep,
  I wrought him more than harm.
I caught him with a tiger's clasp,
I wrung the weapon from his grasp
  And sheathed it to the hilt.
I had no time to think or feel,
My head rang with the clang of steel,
I could not pause for ill or weal,
  To her who stood where blood was spilt.

"I fled. Old time has swiftly rolled
His checkered wheels of gloom and gold,
And tamed the blood that once was bold,
And yet I cannot reason all,
The why such evil did befall.
But this I know, make me as then,
I'd dare all danger. grief or pain.
To live that hour o'er again.
My soul at danger seemed to laugh,
  I feared not man nor gods of old,
I longed this nectared cup to quaff,
  Let it be poison to the soul.

" I did not care to think, for then
I would have slaked my burning thirst,
Though God wrote at the fountain head.
· Beware ! it is accursed, accursed.'
You might as well have sternly told

A wounded, thirsty, dying man
　To pause and not to slake his thirst,
Because another owned the spring—
　Because another drank there first,
As to have quoted in my pain.
‘ Forbidden fruit! refrain, refrain.’

“ The story’s old.　Ah! that is all,
　And nature put it in my mood:
An apple caused two saints to fall—
　The soul will seek the sweetest food.
The fruit was golden ripe and fair.
　So sweet to taste ’twould pay to die.
Though sought it was not found elsewhere,
　Can nature, tell the reason why,
For Nature, father of our will,
　Is Love’s true impulse and its fire;
’Tis Reason that discards the ill,
　And lifts sweet Passion from the mire.
They say there is a heaven above,
　Where tempted not all doeth well.
Here God meant we should live and love—
　We ‘love not wisely, but too well.’ ”

He ceased, and silence brooded then
Awhile o’er camp-fire and o’er glen ;
The musing youth did not reply,
　He deemed the case was stated fair.

He would not banter words, or pry
  Into a grief that had no prayer.
Another, wrapt in sable cloak,
  Drew down his brow with cynic smile,
Essayed to speak, then seemed to choke,
  Then eyed the burning coals awhile,
Then rose erect, with haughty form,
  And gazed into the ether blue,
And shook himself, as in a storm,
  And beat his foot in wild tatoo,
And peering at the arch on high,
Said, "love was never born to die,
But curse us young, and curse us old,
And bind us in the serpent's fold,
And give us guile to be more bold,
And cheat us with its lie.

" I once was young, and good and true,
And walked the paths of virture pure,
  A proud young English nobleman.
Well, when I loved, my nature changed;
The one I loved was cold, estranged,
  And loved another nobleman.
There's nothing strange in that, I'm sure,
And yet it was the devil's lure
  And urged me on to shame.
I sought to slay him from the day
I knew where her affections lay,

And spread a slander on his name.
He was as brave as drew the sword,
And then I sought and got him word
That 'twas another who had said
The thus and so that he had heard—
  A proud young plebian youth,
Whom next she loved for his true worth,
And who adored her on the earth
  Within his noble heart of truth.

" I urged the breach, they met and fought,
  And parried bloody steel with steel;
  At length the nobleman did reel
A deadly thrust he caught;
It pierced him where he buckled belt,
And in his dying blood he knelt—
This was the curse I wrought.
  I waited for her grief to fade,
Then offered her my hand;
  I might as well have sought to stayed
The tide upon the strand
  As to have checked her bitter scorn;
She seemed to read my guilty face
  And brand me as ignoble born,
A fraud, a foul disgrace.

" This stung me to the very quick,
I'd have her now in spite of all.

Some daring knaves I hired then
To seize her in a lonely glen.
   I was to be a hero brave,
And rescue from their power;
   Her plebian lover chanced to save
And shield her in that hour;
I dared not meet his flashing sword,
But rallying then my hired horde
   We pressed him to the wall.
At length his sword fell from his hand
And then o'er powered by our band,
   We caused the hero's fall.

" His gory breast met many shocks,
   But in the silent glen
We piled some lonely scattered rocks
Above the heart that feared no shocks—
   The bravest of brave men.

" Now she was mine I'd have my will
And wreak my vengeance to its fill.
But she was brave. my valiant heart
   Did almost quail before her breath,
She was supreme in virtues part
   And even courted death.
Virtue is strong. Could you behold
   Her lifted hand and flashing eyes.
You'd said the very gods were bold
   To think to claim her for a prize.

"She dared me with a fearless brow
  In presence of the God of gods,
To bow the soul that would not bow
  Against a thousand odds,
She scorned me with a haughty scorn;
  She scoffed me with a coward's name
And bid me slay her ere the morn
  Should look upon her shame.
Great God! She so defied me still,
  Though I adored her charms,
That in the frenzy of my will
  I slew her in my arms."

He paused, and twirled his dark mustache,
And pulled his cloak 'round like a sash,
And bowed his head, and seemed to choke
And then again the silence broke.
" I fled, and on Australia's land
I was a wrecker on the strand.
Thus love hath wrought me worse and worse,
And cursed me with a double curse."

Then spoke the youth with ardent mien
And stirred the coals that glowed between:
" Say not that love hath thus accursed
Thou was't a felon from the first.
And what if thou hadst loved and lost,
Think'st thou that guile could pay the cost?

Think'st thou that crime will ease thy pain.
    And evil is the better way?
Think'st thou we ne'er shall live again
    And love our loves some other day?
Think'st thou the bard that loved and sung
    Along the winding banks of Ayr
Will praise no more with silvery tongue
    The one he loved so fondly there?
Or he who roamed the sea and shore
    And in his deeds and song was bold,
Think'st thou that he will dream no more
    Of her who charmed him to the soul?

" I've scanned the steady flights of time,
    Where truth is strong, and hope can soar
In presence of the sun sublime,
    Where nature spreads her boundless shore.
God's justice points the wheels of time.

" Heaven is, and deathless spirits soar
To where there is a fadeless clime—
    Where suns that rise shall set no more—
Where is a balm for every pain,
    And they that loved shall love again.
There, in the pure and brighter blaze.
    Where far off constellations shine,
They'll walk again love's flowery ways,
    And broken ties will re-entwine.

" But coward felons such as those,
    Before a darker fate shall bow.
Heaven's wrath shall blast such dastards bold
    Who'd dare to mar God's purest gold.
Ye Gods! Shall Heaven's sweetest charm,
    Earth's highest type of truth and grace—
That leans upon man's stronger arm—
    By force or fraud find dark disgrace ?
Use force on woman ?   Lift the might
    Of strength to batter down her right
To virtue and an angel's place ?

" A pyramid of curses, high
As Heaven, shall crush him till he die ;
Like Ixion, hurled to Pluto's shade,
For lawless love where Juno swayed :
He'll welter on tormenting sods,
Through the long æon of the Gods.
Thou art a coward by thy word—
Thou feard'st to meet thy rival's sword,
But dared to do the deed confessed,
" And pierce a helpless woman's breast.

Ye thought to rest here for the night.
Beside my camp-fire blazing bright :
But now thy feet thou canst not rest
Beneath the tent where mine hath pressed.
I doubt not but thou hast a band
Of robbers in this very land!"

Then quick they raised their hands in strife,
And said, " Thy money or thy life !"
And reached to where their weapons lay—
He stopped them ere they reached half-way.
With pistols pointed to their teeth,
He backed them to the wooded heath.
They disappeared within the grove.
He picked, with cautious steps, his way,
And feared the men who sinned for love,
More than the beasts that roamed for prey.

A LEGEND OF THE DELUGE.*

'Mid the isles of the sea, the far Southern Sea,
The sundown of waters whose fair witchery
Blends the flush of the sky with the blue of the sea,
And the heart is as mellow as dates on the tree,

Where they sit 'neath the palm, and the soul is as calm
As their streams that flow soft as the lute to the Psalm,
And love is as sweet as rich incense and balm,
Or the roses that bloom in the vales of Siam.

There a continent smiled, and the sunshine beguiled
The Eden of earth when she first was a child;
But the Deluge was near, when the waters were piled
O'er that Eden now doomed while she dreamt, while she smiled.

On a mountain side bright as the snow on its hight
A hermit dwelt, lone in deep solitude's sight.
In a vale far away spread the gold of sunlight
Where a maiden dwelt, fair as an angel of light.

---

* This legend is supposed to be told by a Montezuma Indian chief, in
which he relates how Montezuma came to earth and brought down the sacred
fire; also, how there came to be a man in the moon. Besides, it is intended
to illustrate love—that grandest theme that has occupied the thought of deity
or man since "God broke the silence of the dead eternities," and ushered
into existence the wonderful creations of his Universe. The stories of this
volume are intended to illustrate Love—its follies and inconsistencies, as well
as its grandeur and beauty.

And the paradise bird paused here in her flight,
And the bul-bul sung in the soft twilight,
And the dodo chattered the morn away,
And life passed on like a summer day.

She loved the lone hermit, but he years before
Had loved a deceiver, and brought to his door
The wreck of a heart and the dream that was o'er ;
He had wooed a deceiver. he'd woo never more.

And the hermit was shy, but the maiden's soft eye
Beamed softly upon him as oft he passed by
From the spring in the vale and cocoa-tree nigh,
Where he sought his provisions and found a supply.

When her love was the strongest she wended her way
To the hut of the hermit at noon of one day,
And the sun was enamored and kissed with his ray
The bloom on her cheek as she passed on her way.

And she said to the hermit : " Come with me I pray
From this lone hut—this doomed earth—come with me to-day.
Father Noah hath filled the old Ark where she lay,
And the beasts, two and two, entered in there to-day.

" I have come as a dove on this mission of love ;
The beasts choose a mate. why not I choose my love?
The preacher of righteousness preacheth his last.
And the floods shall descend with the clouds and the blast."

"Be cursed in thy folly thou simple—thou child !
The heavens are smiling—thy judgment is wild."
His words were too rude for the maiden so mild ;
One moment she trembled, one moment she smiled.

Then she turned in dismay and she fell in despair
From the hight where she stood through the soft yielding air.
Down the side of the mountain the warm sun hung, where
He caught the sweet maiden with long golden hair.

She was gone. Like a star that is sweet to the eye,
Her worth was unknown till she passed from his sky.
He peered down the void, he covered his face—
He shuddered—remorse was as gall to his taste.

But the wise sun was loving and took to his arms
The fairest of maids and the sweetest of charms.
On his bosom she lay and at sunset of day
She spread her gold tresses o'er mountain-tops gray.

Her love was too pure and her heart was too warm
For the chill blasts of earth and the shock of its storm.
There she reigns as a queen, for the times they were then,
When the sons of God sought the fair daughters of men.

And the sun was so warm and the maiden so fair,
So enamored his love and so ardent his prayer,
Montezuma the great was their son and their heir,
And at sunset slid down by her long golden hair,

And brought from that heaven the bright sacred fire
That flames on the altar—earth's great purifier,
And the joy of the world is the love that hath stayed—
As warm as the sun and as pure as the maid.

*　　　*　　　*　　　*　　　*　　　*

Now the stars are awake and a boat skims the lake,
And far muttering thunders the silence doth break.
No breeze stirs a ripple or sighs through the trees,
But sadness broods heavy and moans like the the seas.

And the hermit stepped quickly but sad to the shore.
Where a woman sat weeping with sorrows that pour
On the heart of a woman that but one can adore,
And that one has forsaken, and loves her no more.

Love beamed from his eye and poured from his voice :
" Come, dearest, come weep not, but cause to rejoice
The heart, O. so weary! that sighs for its choice—
The solitude dreary hath spoke but thy voice.

" And the lone years far from thee, like stars in the night,
Held thee warm in my bosom though unseen by my sight.
But a maiden, last noon, as fair as the morn,
Said, 'Come! Earth is drowning,' I answered with scorn.

" But the faith of that maiden, my own faith imbued—
Thou art lone and forsaken—my love is renewed.
Well, I passed the old ark as I came on my way,
She's been building for ages—she's finished to-day.

"There the rabble had brought the old gods from their fane,
While they scoffed the good prophet with tauntings profane.
They had made a bonfire—one snatched a brand out,
Said, 'Come, burn the old temple and hustle them out.'

"When from out a clear sky thunders muttered a curse,
Heaven flashed sudden fire, and threatened far worse;
At that sign from his hand I snatched the red brand,
Hurled it up.—'twas a cloud that o'er shadowed the land.

"Then come to my ark, or my mountain retreat."
But she answered him low with voice sad and sweet:
"He for whom I left you proved untrue, and has fled.
I've blessed him that hath cursed, scorned the true heart that
    bled."

Now the thunders roared dreadful, and deafning their crash,
The lightnings gleam woeful, and lurid their flash;
The earth sinks beneath, the waters heave up,
Heaven pours her dark flood like wine from a cup.

And that continent smiling far in the South sea,
Faded 'neath the drear waters in dark misery;
The ocean above and beneath lost their shore,
And she sank 'neath their bosom to rise never more.

The people fled wildly, but fate's stern decree,
Like hosts of proud Pharaoh whelmed them in the dark sea.
On the top of a mountain two struggled alone,
The last of earth's surface—love's last hopeless throne.

'Mong the people who sought on the day of their doom,
To climb the tall mountains through torrents and gloom;
They scaled it together and hoped through love's prayer,
To o'er come the dark waters, and conquer despair.

But at length o'er the place surged the dark watery waste,
When grasping the girdle that circled her waist.
He reared her above the dark waters awhile,
O'er earth the proud victor, heroic his smile.

Then his soul rose to front the stern judgment of heaven,
Through clench'd lips he muttered "I've long been storm
        driven
On a dark raging sea.   Rage, rage on and smite me,
But Jehovah take her to yon heaven with thee.

" Pour on me thy dark curses, this heart shall ne'er shun,
The fate that's before. till its purpose is won;
Love is stronger than death, it can out last the breath,
'Tis the ark that shall glide o'er eternity's path."

Then he lifted her higher by the lightning's red fire,
She saw a pale drowned face floating nigher and nigher;
'Twas the one who had cursed her with sorrow and woe,
She sprang fondly toward it, and vanished below.

He stood all alone.   The pale moon and proud,
Unvailed the dark waters and peered through a cloud;
The moon was enamored with his courage so true,
She honored his love and she sought for it too.

She caught him up to her, and in her embrace,
He smiles at his folly and laughs in earth's face ;
He that cut down the thorn-tree one calm Sabbath noon,
Is a far different man from the man in the moon.

And he dwells in that heaven, the pale orb of night,
And he smiles on the earth with a calm, sad delight ;
And so melting his glances, so beaming his eye,
The soul of all lovers he fills with a shigh.

For the souls that are lofty are noblest and kind,
And the humblest may love with a love that's divine ;
And if God hath a heaven in the moon, stars or sun,
Love only can win it, if it ever is won.

Footprints and Shadows.

Ah men and sires! ye can not tell
The wealth of woman's love,
The eagle knows his aerie well,
  Nor droops his wings but mounts above.

And o'er it broods with anxious care;
So woman does love's mantle fling,
With softness of the doves that pair,
  And tireless as the eagles wing.

All souls are parcels of one spark divine,
And are as one when bowing at truth's shrine.
All thought, all greatness, since the ages roll,
Is but the upward step, the onward march of soul.
As boys cross stony brooks, from truth to truth afar,
Our souls may to perfection step from star to star.

Dread not decay of age or wrecks of time—
  All hopes, all sorrows shall be thine.
  Be strong and fearless of all fears:
  Think of the bright and countless spheres
  Thy soul shall tread, beyond these cycling years.

WOMAN.

As fragrant flower its sweetness sheds
   Kind woman soothes man's pain and care,
And o'er his darkest pathway spreads
   The sunshine of her smiles so fair.

Methinks, o'er all the realms of space,
   Creative hand ne'er meant to trace
A nobler form, or fairer face,
   With brighter charm, or sweeter grace,

Than woman, who was sent to cheer
   Man in his lonely, hapless fate,
With kindness, and affection's tear,
   And lead him to a higher state.

Her charming face and trusting heart
   Wakes in his breast heroic flame;
For her he toils by strength and art,
   To carve his way to wealth and fame.

He tills the soil, and sails the fleet,
   Subdues the earth, explores its wilds,
To lay his treasures at her feet,
   For her approving love and smiles.

In every land where women stand,
   In loving beauty by man's side,
His rudeness turns to manners bland,
   And truth and honor is his pride.

First at the cradle and the grave,
   With swelling heart and anxious breath,
She ope's the eyes of great and brave,
   And shuts them in the glare of death.

Then tyrant man, that scoffs at fear,
   At your own hearth, or where ye roam.
Strive with true love to bless and cheer
   This angel of our earthly home.

TO VIRGINIA—REMEMBRANCE.

Like dew gems of morning that sparkle so bright,
Like moonbeams adorning the glory of night,
Like visions of beauty, like stars in the main,
Thy image, my fairest, haunts bosom and brain.

Like roses of summer when fairest they bloom,
Like streamlets that murmur 'long banks of perfume,
Like sweet music 'waking, o'er isles in the sea,
Is memory's glance taking bright glimpses of thee.

The hopes that allure me to bliss in the skies,
The promptings that bid me be great and be wise,
Are not in their beauty more pure and more true
Than my heart's fond devotion, my fairest, for you.

Were this world ever bright and fair as it seems,
Were our joys and delight as we paint in our dreams,
They could add no more bliss, as I journeyed along,
Than thy smile and thy presence, thou theme of my song.

TO ETTIE, THE ROSEBUD OF THE HILLSIDE.

I know where lives a pretty maid
　Upon a sunny hillside,
Where summer flowers latest fade,
　And soft zephyrs gently glide.
She is as fair as any flower,
　As pretty as a lily,
Bending from a lovely bower,
　Looking down upon a valley;
She is in her youthful pride:
　She is young, and gay, and pretty,
　And her name is charming Ettie,
The rosebud of the hillside.

And I never saw a maiden
　With a form more lithe and free,
Nor till in the distant Eden
　Do I e'er expect to see
A maid more gay and lively,
　With an eye more softly blue,
And a ringing laugh more lightly,
　Or cheeks of richer hue,
Than those of our blooming pride,
　The young, the gay. the pretty,

With the lovely name of Ettie,
  The rosebud of the hillside.

But thy time is passing, Ettie,
  " Stamp improvement on its wings,"
For the flowers that bloom so pretty
  That the summer gently brings,
Soon do perish, soon are faded,
  And the fairest forms of earth
Death's hand, oftimes unaided,
  Blasts amid their bloom and mirth.
Then. whate'er may thee betide,
  Be thou good, and wise, and pretty,
  Young, light-hearted, charming Ettie,
The rosebud of the hillside.

May thy days be bright and sunny,
  May joys thy heart e'er tune ;
May thy charms mature as bonny
  As the flowers that bloom in June ;
May thy life be long and useful,
  Growing better with thy years,
Till thou bloom on hillsides peaceful—
  In that realm where drops no tears.
Far beyond time's rolling tide,
  Be an angel, pure and pretty,
  Bloom with life immortal, Ettie.
A rose on Eden's hillside.

ETTIE, THE ROSEBUD, HAS PERISHED.

Ettie's dead; she has faded
  Like a flower in its bloom—
Death's cruel hand unaided
  Has laid her in the tomb.
In her bright and smiling beauty,
  Fair and fragile as a lily,
With her winning ways so lovely,
  Shedding fragrance o'er the valley,
She has passed from 'neath the sunlight
  To a narrow chamber lonely,
Darker than the gloom of midnight.
  Yes, our gay and charming pride,
With her face so fair and pretty,
With the lovely name of Ettie,
  Has vanished from the hillside.

I met her in the summer,
  Not many months ago,
When the leaves did sigh and murmur,
  And the zephyrs gently blow.
She asked me, with a sunny smile
  And cheery voice so gay,

If I would write upon her name
  A pretty little lay.
Said I. "with pleasure, charming Ettie,
  If you'll allow a kiss for pay
I will gladly write upon your name so pretty.
  Then she said with charming pride
" If your piece is very pretty
You may get a kiss from Ettie,
  The rosebud of the hillside,"

I never wrote for money,
  I never thought of fame.
But the glowing smile of beauty.
  Oft stirred poetic flame.
I've sometimes loved to sing
  Like the wild bird on the bough,
Just as I felt the swelling song,
  And nature taught me how :
And as it sings where none can hear
  But the silent, sighing trees.
I cared not if it touched the ear.
  Or died upon the breeze.
But I felt with joy and pride
  'Twould be glorious pay, and pretty.
  To obtain a kiss from Ettie.
The rosebud of the hillside.

How short is life. how very brief,
  Even when it slowly closes

In the " sear and yellow leaf:"
But, when fading like the roses,
How deep and dark the grief.
But, oh! sad, indeed, to know,
That, like a tender, fragile lily,
Trying to bud, and bloom, and grow,
She has drooped from off the valley,
And lies buried 'neath the snow.
And it's so o'er all the world so wide;
No flower more fair and pretty
Bloomed with sweeter charm than Ettie,
Yet she faded from the hillside.

They folded her soft, white hands
Upon her snow white breast,
Closed her laughing, bright blue eyes—
Laid her in her coffin to rest.
Dead! Do not speak the word so loud.
Is the bright blooming blossom dead
And folded in her shroud?
And will any think, when they tread
In thoughtless gayety over her head,
That she ever was gay and proud?
Alas! in all this world so wide,
O'er all the fair and pretty,
As well as our charming Ettie,
Death rolls his whelming tide.

She flashed upon our shadowed path,
Like a golden gleam of sunlight—
Like a bright and beauteous star
Glowing in the fields of midnight.
But she's passed to the tearless realm,
Where there's neither night nor gloom—
Where there's fadeless beauty ever,
And naught is laid within the tomb;
Where the tear-drop never glistens,
And the flowers ever bloom.
　　Far beyond time's rolling tide,
As an angel pure and pretty,
Blooms with life immortal, Ettie,
　　Now a rose on Eden's hillside.

LAST WORDS OF STONEWALL JACKSON.

" Let us go across the river and rest beneath the shade of the trees."

Said the good and valiant chieftain, when his battles all were
    o'er,
And his wounded form was lying near the Rappahannock
    shore,
When his body racked with anguish, an his soft eye glanced
    around
At his sad and sorrowing comrades, and the dark and bloody
    ground.
When his pulse beat low and feeble, and his vision seemed
    to fade,
" Let us go across the river and rest beneath the shade."

O the beauty and the pathos of that sad yet soothing thought,
Coming at the end of labors, at the close of battles fought!
Did it cheer the dying soldier, did it light his weary eye,
To behold the bow of promise and the river flowing nigh?
Not the rolling Rappahannock, but death's dark and narrow
    stream,
And the trees of life beyond it, far beyond life's fitful dream.

He was a Christian soldier, with a firm. unfaltering trust,
That the sword he held, and cause espoused, was noble, true
    and just.
No warrior stern, of antique mold, with fierce eye flashing
    keen.
His look was mild as woman's, and gentle was his mien;
Yet, terrible as a thunder-bolt, he rode the battle's crest,
And carnage strewed the vanquished field where'er his cohorts
    pressed.

No warrior clad in glittering steel e'er raised an arm of might,
And struck more quick and stunning blows amid a bloody
    fight:
No eagle eye more quickly saw the point to make a breach.
And startled foemen felt his hand ere they thought themselves
    in reach.
He fought not for fame or love of strife—for war and strife
    he did deplore; '
He struck because he thought he saw invading foemen at his
    door.

Then cherish his noble memory, though sad his fate to tell,
For he sleeps beneath his native shade in the land he loved
    so well.
Though dead, his memory liveth. as chieftain. noble, brave
    and good;
What he deemed was right, he upheld in fight. and like solid
    stone wall stood :

But his spirit has crossed beyond the dark and shadowy
    shore—
Beyond the sun, in the light of God: he needs the shade
    no more.

Let us imitate this chieftain, of a hundred battles fought,
And with firmness, faith and courage, fight our battles as we
    ought:
And when pain and death o'ertake us, and life's stream is
    ebbing low,
And we see the purple twilight, and dark shadows come
    and go,
Let us trust with hope and joy, as life's visions slowly fade,
That we only cross the river to rest beneath the shade

DEATH OF GEN. JOHN C. BRECKINRIDGE.

" Break, break, break," o'er the purple dawn. O day !
  Break in gleams of silver and gold,
For the earth moves on, and the night grows old,
  And scatter the gloom away.

O well for the sun in the morn,
  That it dreads not the heat of the way.
O well for the soul in its earthly toil.
  That it dreams of a brighter day.

For an honored name, and a cherished fame
  Looming bright ere the strength of its noon.
Scarce touched by the blight of a blemish or blame,
  Lost the bloom of its glory too soon.

The gifted of mind. the princely of soul,
  Where genius and honor were one,
Whose fame was enshrined in a nation's heart.
  Hath sank to its setting sun.

The star that arose on the sheen of the West.
  And glowed on the brow of a day that is past,
Whose charm was the pride of a million that bless'd,
  Is gone like the dream of a hope that will last.

And God-given genius. the mystery of mind,
  That sways an electric and unmeasured force,
The fire of the soul, burning bright and refined.
  Have waned in their once brilliant course.

In the lives forgotten, and the immortal few,
  Something unfinished remain,
And genius, and learning, and greatness, and fame,
  Promise that which they ne'er can attain.

For the laurel will fade, and the brow where it laid,
  And the ear grow dull to its praise,
And the noblest form lie at rest in the shade,
  Unmindful of marble its glory may raise.

Soar, soar, soar, thou spirit uncaged from clay !
  Soar to a dome on the golden shore,
Where suns never set at the close of the day,
  And souls are at home ever more.

And the spirit heard, and it said to the clay.
  " Go thou to thy chamber of rest !"
And the brow grew pale and cold where it lay.
  And the heart ceased to beat in the breast.

And the eye that was bright, lost the glow of its fire,
  The arms lay unnerved on the breast,
And the tongue that was silvery as songs of the lyre,
  Were stilled in their long dreamless rest.

O sad that the hand that was honored and true,
    And the heart that was noble should fail,
And sink in the dull nerveless grasp of the earth,
    Till they mingle with clods of the vale.

O well for the arm when its strong in its grasp,
    And the heart beats bravely and gay,
That they dread not the chill of that chamber of gloom,
    That lies just before—at the end of the way.

Soon, soon, soon, did the hero, the statesman we mourn,
    Early in fame, and his silent turn,
Take up the pale march to the far-off bourn
    Where hands ne'er weary, and hearts never burn.

Then silent and mournful lay him to rest,
    No boom of cannon to speak of the past.
No sigh of furled banners above his cold breast,
    No sound, but heart beats where remembrance will last.

Break, break, break, thou light of an endless morn!
    Though clouds obscure that we cannot see,
We know thou wilt break o'er a soul high-born.
    In the realms of eternity.

Gone, gone, gone, is the light of a noble eye,
    And the grasp of a genial hand ;
But beyond the night there breaks the light,
    On a soul in the better land.

CENTENNIAL THANKS.

Thank heaven! we have a broad domain
Of blooming vales and fertile plain
Extending fair from main to main,
   In our blest land of liberty.
No sceptered king to rule and reign,
No galling yoke or slavish chain,
But man is free to strive and gain,
   And monarch of his destiny.

Thank heaven! we have a glorious past
Of noble deeds, where strife has cast
No fatal shadows, doomed to last
   And blast our future glory.
United by the sacred ties
Of blood, and common hopes that rise,
Our future bright with starry skies
   Shall glitter in the minstrel's story.

Thank heaven! our land renews its life,
Our country's free from civil strife
Peace reigns where passion once was rife,
   In common brotherhood and unity.
No longer plunging in the fray
The blue commingle with the gray,

But all with gladness hail the day
   Of true allegiance to our country.

Thank heaven! there are brave hearts and true,
God knows them as the world ne'er knew.
And men that dare to think and do,
   And fear no tyrant's prison bars.
And there are souls, meek souls and wise,
Some in frail bodies of small size,
Some hunch-back, bowed, that in God's eyes
   Are taller than the red ripe stars.

Thank heaven! religion lights our sod
And points us where Redeemer trod,
And here reveals to man, his God,
   His nature and his destiny.
And like all conquering cohorts press
The march of mind, with keenest zest,
To make man's earthly home more blest,
   And solve time's every mystery.

And deep in ocean's rocky bed,
O'er monsters, and forgotten dead,
Warm thoughts from living breasts are sped,
   Electric as the lightning's pour.
And land seems nearer unto land,
And hand is closer stretched to hand
In commerce, and the world doth stand
   Close neighbors talking at their door.

Thank heaven! our chivalry can prove
We trust and honor woman's love
A heritage of heaven above,
    A benediction on our history.
Thank heaven! we take a nobler stand
Than in the orient Harem Land,
Where she's the chattel of the man
    Who traffics in her destiny.

Here she may show her brow of snow,
Her dimpling cheeks, and eyes that glow,
And unattended smiling go,
    Unveiled, unmasked without a fear.
And every freeman's willing arm,
A ready shield from wrong and harm,
Her presence, heaven's living charm,
    And manhood scarce her noble peer.

*   *   *   *   *   *   *   *   *

Then trust our nation's future shocks
Shall leave her firm as Corinth's rocks ;
And Phœnix like to ne'er expire,
But rise renewed from every fire,
And build enduring art and fame
More potent than Athenas' name,
Empurpled Tyre, or seven hilled Rome,
Or Babylon in her ancient home ;
Enduring as the earth and stars,
Unhurt by fraud, unslain by wars.

THE DAY COMETH, ALSO THE NIGHT.

Turn, turn O wheel of cycling Time!
   Turn 'round and 'round O wheel of Fate!
Bring flowers from the summer clime;
   Bring treasures from the golden gate
Of sunset seas.   And more than these
   Bring blooming roses to the cheek.
Let laughter ripple on the breeze,
   For youth is gay. and love will speak,
And day is but the span of light,
Proclaiming there will be a night.

Turn 'round O wheel of fortune turn!
   All things move in a cycle strange;
A cradle—then a solemn urn,
   And down the mystic groves of change,
A varied lesson all must learn.
   Life passes like a shuttle's flight,
A little span of day between
   The shadows of the coming night.
And darkness where it first was seen.

All things move in a cycle strange ;
   The ripple of the laughing rill,
The dew drop on the mountain range ;
   The cloudlet floating o'er the hill,

Are but the varied steps of change.
  The seasons whirl through flowers and frost,
From icy Winters come the Springs,
  The forms that change are never lost.
Can matter have such subtle wings;

And yet the soul, once God's own breath,
  Built up and shaped by his right hand,
Must it pass through the shadow death,
  To find beyond no Border Land?
Must that which gives to matter life,
  And moulds it like the potter's clay,
While matter lasts through change and strife,
  Must it's proud master fade away;
Or like the bird uncaged and free,
  Soar to bright worlds of destiny?

Life has its day; its sombre night,
  Then comes another fairer day,
Else why the angel hopes that write
  Their sweet dreams o'er our earthly way?
From heaven's far off jeweled towers,
  God hangs the stars like banners bright,
And in the silent whispering hours,
  His voice is in their beams of light.
Ye weary toilers on life's road!
  Ye burdened hearts so strong and true—
Patience, a step, death lifts the load,
  And angel wings will come for you.

THE PAST AND FUTURE.

The years have rolled their days of gold
　　Along the path of time,
While shimmering through the amber fold
　　Of skies that bend sublime,
The sun from out his hights of old
　　Rides through his azure clime,
And stirs the blaze upon his hearth
To warm the circling face of earth.

Who forged the fires upon his crest,
The burnished armor on his breast,
　　And sent him forth like knight of old,
　　With dazzling shield of brightest gold
Where day spreads forth her ambient sheen
With space of darkness stretched between,
　　And day and night, and gloom and light
　　Wheel in their grooves of endless flight?
Where goes he with his martial host
Of glowing orbs whose grandest boast
　　Is that amid its cohorts far
　　Upon a tempest driven star,
There lives and treads its rock-ribbed crust
A reasoning atom built of dust?

God rules and marshals all so well,
They feel his wise mesmeric spell:
  "Let there be light." Light did appear
  And worlds gazed on a sun-lit sphere.

And earth can whirl, and stars can sing,
And time fly on a tireless wing
  Ten thousand times, ten thousand years,
  Regardless of man's smiles or tears.
A million hearts that bow and mourn,
A thousand worlds by earthquakes torn,
  Is but the programme to that bourn;
  What bourn? God knows. The end of years,
The summing up of time and tears.
When earth and time shall be no more,
  And souls like suns, shall shine and soar.

The Past is but a name for Fate,
Those hieroglyphics on the gate
  Of all the ages—what are they?
  A dream that had a living day.
Go view the pyramids awhile;
Read, if thou canst, the Syhinx's smile
Forever gazing on the Nile,
  Untie the Gordian knot, and see
  The Sybil's dream of destiny;
And if thou hast the wizzard sight
To turn earth's shadows into light,

Tell of the hundred gated Thebes,
The crumbling shrines like autumn leaves
That strew the past.   Of Memnon grand,
Where Ammon strews the desert sand;
    Unriddle all the fabled lore
    Of Egypt and the Sanscrit store.

Earth's blazing altars, where are they?
One varied chapter marks their day
    From Druid's elm and Juggernaut,
    Where Moloch's heated image wrought
Destruction to its votaries.
In superstition's blackening breeze
    Blind devotees have blindly striven
    To propitiate offended heaven.
From Delphian oracles to hights
Where Baal taught debasing rites,
    And Astoreth held her court of lust,
    And Mizraim worshipped reptile dust,
Man has bowed down to lowest sod,
And worshipped some false, unknown god;
    Few knowing of the flame divine.
    Love's gospel, writ at Christian's shrine.

War's common history covers all,
From Nineveh to Plevna's fall;
    Earth's kings and warriors of renown
    O'er bleaching bones marched to a crown.
And few like Xerxes wept to know

Their millions soon would march no more.
  Hannibal, Cæsar, names that shine,
  And Alexander, slain by wine;
Alaric, curse and scourge of man,
  And monsters such as Zingis Khan,
  And Nero, and a thousand more
Were chiefly great in human gore.
And cities sacked and maiden slaves,
  And wives wronged o'er their husband's graves,
  Is justice such as ages find
Man metes out to his fellow kind.

The Future, who can tell? To me
'Tis synonym of destiny.
  Yet this we know: Each heart shall bear
  Some faded dream, some cross of care
From out the flight of waning years,
And flowers of hope bedewed with tears
  Shall bloom for all. And we shall see
  O'er mountain hight and sunset sea,
A prophecy of coming light,
Beyond the gloom that shades the night.
Earth is not a lone orphan star;
God's eye is on her from afar,
  She dances on beneath his gaze,
  While Autumns smile, and Summers blaze,
And seasons tread their round of flowers,
And mellow suns chase golden hours.

THE MINSTREL'S FAREWELL.

The harp is silent, still its strings
Vibrating o'er the spirit flings,
The soul-touch of its lingerings,
    The echo of its minstrelsy.
Long ages since creation rang
And all the stars of morning sang,
Still, they in dropping beauty hang,
    A song to all eternity.

If it shall cause one soul to seek
And prize the flush on beauty's cheek,
And sun his soul in love and speak
    New life to its immortal fire;
'Tis not in vain his harp he strung,
    'Tis not in vain the minstrel flung,
Some heart-drops from his bosom wrung,
    Upon his trembling untaught lyre.

Love was his motto, love his theme,
Fantastic was its wandering beam,
And shadows fitted through its dream
    The wonders of its mystery.
'Twas sad : 'twas gay : it taught to pray :
'Twas beauteous as the flowers of May ;

It wished to stay, to fly away,
   God knows alone its history.

Like harp Æolian ; good and true,
God's winds must blow him through and through,
'Till polished like a drop of dew,
   Who dares the flights of minstrelsy.
Who hath the great magician touch,
That souls entranced may wonder much,
At new creations grandly such,
   Must tune and strike it fearlessly.

Who nobly does, must nobly think,
The soul that soars can never sink,
And man 's a strange connecting link,
   Between frail dust and Deity.
A starlight straying through the gloom,
A flower blooming o'er the tomb,
A spirit fearless of all doom,
   Is his blest immortality.

Life's span is short, and duties throng,
Like steel-clad warriors deft and strong,
And who would wake persuasive song,
   Before a critic callous world.
Perchance some note of simple strain,
May cheer the heart that's sad with pain,
Then silence and oblivion reign,
   Sole victors. with their banners furled.

To be a while like those who've died,
To tread the earth and see its pride,
To mix where strife and mammon vied.
    If his and duty's chivalry.
Yet knows like Druid sad and lone,
Or Santon in his hut of stone,
This earth, though 'twere a diamond throne,
    Is not worth half its rivalry.

Joy stirred the song, ambitions grand.
And fancy spread her rainbow land.
And sorrow took him by the hand,
    So varied is life's fleeting spell.
It led him where the sunlight fades,
Beside the gloomy Stygian shades,
Where dust is heaped with silent spades,
    And lips sigh back no last farewell.

Like eagles that in silence bow
On lonely crag, or mountain brow,
He's watched with kind indifferene, how
    The world's great play goes bravely on.
Hopes banners wave with tears wet through,
Pride struts, and merit lacks her due,
The many toiling for the few,
Dim starlight and the circling sun.

He saw the bows, and meek salaams.
Of fawning hearts, that strewed their palms,

Before the shoddy tinseled shams
  Of fiction's base and timbreled lies.
And slavish knees that bent to pride,
And banded pelf, and theft whose stride,
Was giant-like, and heaven defied,
And few avenge, and none despise.

But none are perfect, no not one,
There's even spots upon the sun,
And few life's checkered course can run,
  Who hath no need of charity.
Life's joys too, like her years are few,
Between the thorns the rose peeps through,
And little pleasures like the dew,
  Best soften its asperity.

Learn to forgive; thy frailties own ;
Forgiveness never had been known,
Had man ne'er sined, law stood alone,
  And mercy first was found in heaven.
Of which bold Lucifer ne'er dreamed,
Nor fallen seraphim.   O'er them gleamed
Unpardoning wrath ; and such they deemed
  Man's fate from Eden driven.

O'er God's grand temple doth entwine
This law.   *He rules by right divine*
Who rules by love.   Thus he doth define
  The tyranny of sceptered power.

Home is man's kingdom.   'Neath its wing
Sweet comforts smile and pleasures sting —
There every man's a patriarch king,
  With jeweled empress and loves dower.

He scanned the past from early dawn,
The world slow marching on and on,
The Present, like a giant born,
  That leaps strong-armed into the fray.
No hoary wizard harper he,
And yet the future, like a sea,
Spread on his sight, the grand *to be*,
  Ere time shall close her hastening day.

When earth shall throb with aching breast,
From swarming vale to mountain crest
With myriad souls ; and life the test
  Of science mixed with toil and tears.
Man's brotherhood shall close the wars,
With policy and cunning jars,
And knowledge front the solemn stars,
  And learn the mystery of the years.

Like pilgrims on Sahara's strand,
Who chase a mirage o'er the sand,
And grasping, find but dust in hand,
  And cheated fall across their graves ;
The simoon on life's desert plain,
The strife for bliss we do not gain,

The blight of hope, the sting of pain ;
  But sweeten death's cold chilling waves.

Harp of the soul! thy cords are strung
By the hand of Fate. Life's song is sung
'Twixt smiles and tears, from the stars among,
  To the dusky depths vibrating.
While the world's at play, the world so gay,
And few will pause to think or pray,
Till passions' clamor ends the day,
  Where a dreamless night is waiting.

In the bliss to be, the soul is free,
And the hand of Fate by the crystal sea,
No more can tune thy minstrelsy
  In the isles of the far off shore.
But they'll waft their songs with a sweet refrain,
To hearts that moan like the sobbing main,
'Till they fear no pain, but climb to gain
  The peerless hights where the soul can soar.

The echoes die, the harp is still,
Its cadence hath no power to thrill,
'Twas music caught from yonder rill,
  'That sunbeams kissed and let it fall.
It came, it went—its music blent
With shadows of the firmament,
The end is *silence.* God hath meant
  That SILENCE soon shall come to all.

Aristophanes, W. J. Hickie

The Comedies of Aristophanes

A New and Literal Translation From the Revised Text of Dindorf...